CRYSTAL E. GREEN

Lavender Lily

To Marvin, the love of my life.
To Marleigh, the incredible version of myself that I was never quite confident enough to be.
To Mason, my amazing package full of rarities.
And to those who've never stopped believing.
Thank you.

"Even lavender lilies wither sometimes."

— Ivory Eloi

Contents

Preface

I often wonder if I've gone too far. I anxiously examine the facts buried inside Lauren's fiction as I struggle to shake the annoying assumption that they are so far-fetched, you won't believe her story. Or that you won't believe mine - which of course, is the very basis of this one. Though my worries are beyond the realms of my control, I do wonder. But I have come to accept a universal truth - that at one point or another, each of us experiences the waves of life in ways that no one could have imagined or prepared us for. So, I leave you with *Lavender Lily* - the unbelievable story of a young, blossoming woman whose life took turns she never saw coming. A story of relentless love, unbreakable bonds and vulnerability – through and through.

Born from my original screenplay, *Lock the Door* —a psychological thriller inspired by my experience with postpartum depression and the misdiagnosed days that followed— *Lavender Lily* dives deeper into the life and mind of the protagonist and those who love her the most. May the pages ahead inspire you to see the light. May they soften your heart to an alternate possibility. And may they remind those who doubt the director that their judgment is uncalled for.

Matters of maternal mental health have been brought into question since the very conception of this work. I have read countless critiques from those enraged by how the media portrays mothers postpartum and I have been personally criticized for the role I choose to play in it. My heart holds space for those who have been misunderstood and for those who still fear the ramifications of releasing the stigma, and I am without uncertainty that this work will set more fuel to that flame. But the fact of the matter is that sometimes our minds play tricks on us. And sometimes, we are let in on the secret; other times, we are not.

But regardless of the possibilities or the probabilities, I will never back down from the truth… from *my* truth. That as beautiful and powerful as motherhood is, it isn't easy, it isn't always fun, oftentimes it hurts like hell and despite whatever label(s) the professionals assign you, some feelings and emotions simply cannot be elucidated. Moreover, some of those feelings and emotions have less to do with motherhood and more to do with the veins of human nature that some of us aren't yet prepared to expose. So, I invite you to take *Lavender Lily* for what it is: One woman's story. One woman's fight. And one woman's picture of perfection shattered into pieces that *one* time she lost control. But she isn't the only one now, is she?

1

The Consultation

I remember the day as if it were yesterday. I had just finished tidying the office after recovering from an hour-long session with "Jealous Jessie," as I had privately nicknamed him. He was a middle-aged, Mexican-American martial artist from Minnesota who had neglected his thriving career and moved to the Southeast to keep eyes on his newly married ex-wife, who had determined that she'd had enough of his jealous ways. So, it came as no surprise to me that a swiftly acquired restraining order along with a requirement for anger management had landed Jessie a series of psychotherapy sessions with me. I wasn't the most affordable of the therapists in the area, but when reaching the root of an issue was the primary obstacle, *everyone* knew who to call. No, I'm not bragging; however, I am very aware of what I bring to the table and I welcome the casual contester's point of view any day of the week, really.

As I glanced over her file, my mind played with the possibilities for her appointment. We could all benefit from the work of a counselor or therapist at some point in our lives, but "why would a woman of her status require a seat on *my* sofa?" I wondered just before I opened the door and welcomed her inside.

She was the most fascinating person I had ever encountered, client or otherwise. On the outside, she was *remarkably* stunning. Her chestnut-coated skin elegantly enveloped inside her carefully cultivated couture. Her unapologetic coils placed ever so gracefully around her flawlessly framed face. Her confidence, her poise and her smile. All unmistakably... *perfect.* Her bold brown eyes, however, spoke a complex inner truth that poor Lauren's lips were never quite brave enough to release.

From the moment she first stepped foot inside my office, I knew that both Lauren and I were in for a ride. Where to? I wasn't quite sure. But I trusted my instincts, and the weight of her burdens bullied me further outside my comfort zone than I had ever been before. And it didn't take long for me to realize that I was no longer behind the wheel... if I ever was.

"Lauren Ivory Winters," she proudly announced, in a tone as rasp as it was regal, as I inquired about her intentions.

"You know, my mother always says that real women keep real secrets," she giggled, "but I'll tell *you*, Dr. Lewis... I'm thirty-three. There, I said it."

I smiled and took notes as I listened to what sounded like scripted responses to interview questions that no one had ever even asked. Why on Earth had she really come to see me? And why the fuck did being in her presence make me feel so goddamned... *uneasy?*

Those were the real questions I had. Hell, I already knew her name. I, like most people, was already well aware of what she did for a living, who she was married to and how much their home cost. And a quick Google search provided every other minute detail of her life. Details that, for the purposes of psychotherapy, didn't move the needle one bit. In fact, they were utterly useless pieces of the puzzle that didn't seem to affect the big picture.

In a way, her performance was like being on a date with a beautiful man whose sole intention was to impress me. Sure, that would be pleasant at first, but after a while, I would wish for more than smiles, assurances and stories of his successes. I wouldn't care about his former lovers, how he preferred his eggs cooked or how many children his great Aunt Linda gave birth to during the Great Depression. I imagine I would find those details both premature and less than pertinent to a proper introduction.

In other words, I was rather bored with Lauren and felt forced to sit and absorb an abundance of bullshit when in real life, I would have much rather been getting my car washed and waxed at the new spot on 79th and Lennox. You know, the one with the baby blue archway and the dual entry with the fluorescent peacock decor. Perhaps I'm biased because I absolutely adore birds, but it's tasteful, they were running a grand opening special and it's only two blocks away from my favorite restaurant, Lavender Lily's. I love their couscous stir fry, and I always add on a side of seared Sockeye. Oh, and a small salad! You should try it sometime - if you haven't already.

But rather than allow my personal feelings to jeopardize three decades' worth of prestige and professionalism, I did what any good therapist would do: I listened as she filled my ears with elaborate accounts of her achievements as an accomplished author from Auburn, how she exceeded her parents' expectations and quickly rose to the top of her graduating class at Spelman College an entire year and a half before her advisor's predictions. How she initially committed to being a neurosurgeon but decided against it because math and science weren't quite her thing. And how she had personally designed every little detail of her wedding ceremony decades before she even had a suitor.

But after fifteen pages of notes that seemingly had nothing to do with anything that mattered, I slowly raised my right index finger, just like *my* mother did whenever she needed to excuse herself from the congregation to use the bathroom, spank my bottom or have a bite of the sausage biscuit she kept tucked inside her purse because we were always running late for church. And she would rather snack between songs and scriptures than be titled tardy. Come to think of it - I never did quite understand why my mother raised that finger. Not as a young girl and certainly not now. Who exactly was she seeking approval from? And did she think that by not lifting that finger to excuse herself, the man in the pulpit might make her take her seat? I digress.

"Pardon me, Lauren," I eventually interrupted.

"Yes?" she softly answered.

"Thank you for that information," I said. "I am so sorry to cut you off mid-sentence, but you seemed rather distraught when you called into my office requesting a consultation this morning. But now, you seem quite the opposite. I'm curious. What changed?"

"Oh, that," she said as she chuckled to herself. "No, I am perfectly fine, Dr. Lewis. I guess I just got a little overwhelmed with the baby, and my best friend, Gina, and my husband, Greg, suggested I see someone. That's all. I'm fine, really."

"Hm," I uttered as Lauren's meticulously manicured fingernails fidgeted against her tightly clenched clutch.

"Are you sure, Lauren?" I queried as tears began to puddle over her pupils.

She lowered her head and closed her eyes as thick tears dripped down onto her lap, reminiscent of rain tapping against a rooftop on a gloomy day. And the most spine-chilling seven minutes of my life ensued as a languid Lauren hummed a hair-raising rendition of "Hush Little Baby" while she rocked herself back and forth against the cushions of my couch. Once again, my instincts were right. Lauren was *far* from fine.

"Lauren, are you still in there?" I questioned as I nervously slid to the edge of my chair, knowing good and well that the person sitting across from me was not the same person who had walked into my office.

I had seen file cabinets full of phobias, fears and failed friendships throughout the course of my career, but this… this was something else entirely. And for the first time in my entire adult life, urine trickled down my thighs as the stranger sitting across from me leaned forward, cracked her knuckles and grinned.

"I don't give a damn what none of the others told you about me!" she declared.

As the moisture in my panties grew cold, my heart nearly beat itself out of my chest. I had gone from sheer boredom to a state of bewilderment in the split of a second, and in that moment, I was petrified as this striking young woman *showed* me exactly why my services were necessary. Though I was afraid that I lacked the skills needed to deliver us from this evil, I held on to hope, because although my life felt complete, I was not prepared for my conclusion.

"*Who*, Lauren?" I managed to ask as she reached into her

clutch, pulled out a Montecristo Number 4, lit it, took a long steady draw and blew the smoke directly into my nostrils. "Who are the others?"

"You think I don't know, Doctor? You think I don't know how you feel about me?!" she exclaimed as she stood up out of her seat and began to stroll around my office.

My blouse and back became one as sweat rapidly poured from my pores, and my voice, suddenly lost as her raging hands raked across floating shelves, destroying retro replicas, frames filled with fantasies and friends and knickknacks that the Rwandan designer I hired picked up because he felt like they brought a sense of serenity to the space. So much for serenity, Olivier. So much for serenity!

"I've worked my ass to the bone to get where I am!" she roared as she gripped her crotch with one hand and lowered the cigar from her lips with the other, her voice harshened by her heavy inhalations. "No way in hell I'm letting you, a damned kid or the next motherfucker take it all away from me! Fuck that!" she exclaimed.

I cleared my throat as I attempted to take control of the situation.

"Uh, Lauren—" I managed to insert before she shut me up.

"Bitch, I swear to God, you got one more time to call me by her name," she said.

"Well, what… what should I ca-call you then?" I stuttered.

"What the hell else would you call me?" she asked as she chuckled.

"I'm Larry!" she announced as she smashed her cigar straight into the wall.

In that moment, I questioned every single thing that I had ever believed in. I wasn't quite sure how the next seventeen minutes of our session would play out, but there was no doubt in my mind that life was over for me. I knew it was. As mental health professionals, we are taught not to use the term "crazy" when referring to our clients. You know, so they never feel worse than they are already feeling. For empathy's sake. But now, with my life on the line and a stranger in my house, my mind only had the potential to formulate one clear thought: this bitch is crazy!

"Aye, aye, aye," she said as she nearly knocked over the most expensive vase in the room. "Where are my manners?" she innocently asked herself as she turned and trotted toward me, extending one hand to me while fluffing her hair with the other.

I don't know when it happened, but once again, *something* had changed. Her voice. It was… different. The way she pronounced the most common words - the confidence in her tone. And there was now a peculiar accent. Colombian, I think. The way her hips swayed from side to side as she crossed the room with a sense of cool and a spirit of sophistication. The way she scoffed me off when my wimpy handshake didn't satisfy her need for something that I was apparently unequipped to provide.

"What's your problem, honey?" she asked as she turned and returned to her seat. "You sit there with that silly look on your face like I'm not supposed to be here or something. Well, my money is just as good as anybody else's money, alright? I didn't come here for all of this. You don't wanna shake my hand? Then, just say that and I'll leave you alone."

"Lauren?" I questioned.

"Oh," she grunted as she rolled her eyes throughout her head then proceeded to pull a tube of red lipstick from her clutch.

And no, not that modest red that wholesome women wear when they've reached a certain age that they dare not disclose. This was *red*-red. It was sexy, shameless and enticing.

"That's what this is about," she said. "It's not your fault. I get it - Lauren… Carmen, they're similar. Right? I can't even begin to tell you how many times strangers have approached me on the street, begging for *her* autograph."

I didn't know what to think or how to feel.

"It's comical, really," she laughed.

"But I just sign that bitch's name on their hats or shirts or whatever they want," she admitted. "They don't know the difference. And… and Lauren, she's pathetic! She has no idea how good she has it, and she would rather cry and complain than pick up that pretty face of hers and carry the fuck on. That's what I do when my life gets out of order."

I stared on in both shock and admiration. On the one hand, I was terrified but grateful that Larry had given me a second chance at life. But on the other hand, I was impressed at the seamless switch between Larry and Carmen in just a matter of seconds.

"Carmen?" I asked as she faced herself in a pocket mirror and smoothed the lipstick over her lips. "Do you *know* Lauren?"

"Of course I do," she replied. "Well, I don't *know her*-know her, but I know everything I need to know."

"She mentioned that she'd gotten overwhelmed with her baby," I said, "and that her best friend and her husband suggested she come see me. Do you know anything about that?".

She clapped the mirror shut, stuffed it inside the clutch, crossed her legs and pouted her bright red lips to perfection.

"Listen to me, honey," she said. "A real man would never

leave his woman alone to care for a whining baby while he's out running the streets doing who knows what with God knows who. So whatever the hell it is that she's been telling you about her man, don't believe it. Everybody knows that he's a good one, and to tell you the truth, I don't know what he sees in her. That's all I'll say about that."

I took notes, but more than anything else, I was ready to retire.

"Hadn't I helped enough people?" I thought to myself.

I, like Lauren, had graduated early and at the top of my class. I entered this field because I enjoyed guiding people who had lost their way in life and simply needed the motivation to get back on track. But not in this way! In less than one hour, I had witnessed one woman become three, and I knew, without a shadow of a doubt, that all I really had to offer her was a prescription or a referral to the nearest psychiatric facility because being *one* Black woman in America was hard enough as it was. Still is.

But when I lifted my head this time, my heart sank into my stomach. And all of my insecurities soon drifted out the door as the beautiful woman who had come into my office claiming overwhelm sobbed without control. She looked deflated, almost as if she had made it back down to the bottom of a mountain she had never intended to climb.

"Dr. Lewis, the truth is that ever since my son was born," she said, "I haven't felt very much like myself. I'm so lost, and some days I forget where I am or what I've done. Life was good for me, you know?! I had everything a woman could dream of having. The love, family, friends, money and career fulfillment that most people spend their whole lives pretending to have. But it's been months since I've written anything, and when I look in the mirror, sometimes it feels like a stranger is looking back at me. Dr. Lewis, can you help me?" she begged.

Poor Lauren. She *needed* me. It *was* women like her that I had signed up to help! Not Larry or Carmen or whomever the hell else was haunting her. But how the fuck was I, with cold piss sticking to my inner thighs and a wet spot on my back the size of Texas, going to pull that off? I wasn't sure, and I couldn't believe that I was thinking this, but I wanted to give it my best shot.

The hour was up, and I was about to release the *real* Lauren back into the world, because God only knows that there's no more room behind bars for brokenhearted Black mothers or their stray sons who will one day grow up without them. So, that's what I did, and my fear of Lauren and her son's future lingered like Larry's secondhand smoke. No matter where I was or what activities I was engaged in, thoughts of Lauren swallowed me, and my decision to set her free, each time I did, left a lump of uncertainty in my throat.

I became so obsessed with saving Lauren from herself that I began spending every moment of my free time researching outpatient treatment facilities, suspected diagnoses and historical cases of psychosis and mania. My initial assumption was that she suffered from postpartum depression or another related postpartum mood disorder. But her symptoms soon revealed a conglomerate of conditions that I couldn't quite classify as one or the other. And I'm ashamed to admit that I began monitoring her movements or, in other words, stalking her. I could never live with myself if my refusal to admit Lauren backfired and the only way I could control that narrative was to keep a close watch. I terminated all other client relations, and my sole focus became Lauren Ivory Winters.

I suppose I saw pieces of myself in every part of her. Pieces that I had either neglected or had forgotten existed, pieces that I envied and wished for myself. And pieces that felt true to who I was at that moment… a hypocritical hybrid of a human, or so I felt.

2

The Ceremony

Most wives-to-be spend months planning the perfect wedding - rummaging through countless bridal magazines and pinning pictures of cookie-cutter color schemes, blush blue bouquets and carefully crafted chignons —that feel right at the time but all wrong as time passes— to boards born one minute and buried the next because nothing ever really feels special enough until you find it. But I, for one, felt very fortunate because I had only ever *heard* or read about those experiences. I have *always* known exactly what I wanted my wedding day to be like, but more importantly, years of watching my mother turn wishful thoughts into dreams come true showed me exactly what I *didn't* want my special day to be like.

"'Lavender lilies, lush green trees and a bright blue sky surround a modern masterpiece,'" I wrote in my wedding journal at just seven years old.

Because even then, the idea of trusting trends to determine my personal taste was a turnoff. I know, I sound just like her. But what can I say? I *am* my mother's child.

As a young girl, I watched as my mother, Robin, the most sought-after dress designer in the state, hand-stitched the most gorgeous gowns that most people, including my young self, had ever seen, in person or otherwise. She placed jewels where jewels were usually forbidden, splits that lifted Southern grandmothers from their graves and controversially creative cuts that became known around town as "The Robin". And still, to this very day, I have never seen a gown that compares in quality, craftsmanship or flair. That woman is incredibly gifted and I am sincerely grateful to call her mine. But I must warn you: if you compliment her work, she will dominate *at least* the next three hours of your time, telling you decades-old tales of her rise from clueless country girl to the woman she was destined to become. Trust me on this one. Yes, you will leave the conversation drained but, nevertheless, inspired.

But thanks to my mother, I have fingered some of the *finest* fabrics in the world, sniffed flowers that smelled like fancy fragrances and there isn't a shade or hue on fad that I am not already well accustomed to. So when Greg asked me if I thought we should hire a planner for our wedding day, I kissed him twice then kindly asked him to keep that money in the bank because there were a billion and one other ways I could think to spend it.

When our special day came, everything turned out exactly as I had envisioned when I was a little girl, just a bit more grown-up, of course. The lavender lilies, the lush green trees, the bright blue sky *and* the modern masterpiece - my every wish had been granted! My favorite cousin, Denise, even agreed to sing at our wedding, which made it all the more special and, indeed, memorable. I used to beg Denise to sing 'You Don't Know My Name' every time my Aunt Vickie, my father's baby sister, brought her over for a sleepover. You remember that song, don't you? It was my *favorite* song back in the day, and Denise used to put her own spin on it and harmonize over the track with Alicia Keys. And my eyes would always water whenever she started singing because songs and the beautiful voices that sang them had a way of penetrating my soul like nothing else ever did.

I was too embarrassed to admit that I was crying because I was overwhelmed with emotions, so I would lie and say that my allergies were acting up! Can you believe that? Don't tell Denise, but I've never really been allergic to anything. And you would think that I would have picked up on something with both of my parents having peanut intolerances and two of the worst cases of seasonal allergies their doctor has ever treated.

Anyway, back to the ceremony! As I was upstairs getting dressed, I held back most of my tears as I heard Denise's soulfully romantic vocals welcoming our guests into our lovely home. Yes, that modern masterpiece belonged to Greg and I, which meant that we could designate venue funds to an exclusive honeymoon in Mauritius - another one of my dreams. Despite my parents' success, they raised me in an incredibly modest house. But I don't suppose I've ever been a modest girl.

"This is *our* dream home, baby girl," my father, Kenneth, would always tell me when I complained about the lack of closet space in my bedroom. "When you grow up, you'll pick out your own," he would say.

And I could not wait! Looking back, I had more than enough closet space to accommodate my belongings. I just didn't have enough room for all of the belongings I had yet to acquire. To ease my anxiety, I covered my bedroom walls with magazine clippings of outfits I'd coordinated myself, shoes years ahead of me and minks made for women twice my mother's age. I've always had a thing for vintage and I've always made it look like the next best thing.

So when the time came for us to buy our first home together, we didn't hold back. I don't mean to boast, but it was perfect. The kitchen was fully equipped with cherry oak cabinetry, high-end stainless steel appliances and a long granite island blended just beautifully to create an immaculate chef's paradise. Naturally, it was the best place to host our wedding, so that's exactly what we did.

As I walked down our spiral staircase —the twinkle from our classic crystal chandelier illuminating my skin— I felt more confident than I had ever felt about anything in my whole life. My proud father smiled as I gracefully made my way down the stairs toward him. My feet were warm and my heart was pure without a doubt or fear. In my mind, there was nothing to second guess. Greg was my soulmate, and I could tell by the look in my father's eyes that he knew it, too. I felt like such a lucky girl.

My lace train swayed across the floral runner and my beaded ivory gown selfishly hugged every curve of my femininely fit frame. And thanks to my grandmother, Ivory, rest her soul, there were *many* curves. Her pearl and blue diamond necklace adorned my collar; the beaming sunshine invaded every window in the room, married its' sparkle and created a coincidental glow upon my face. I felt like a royal queen as I entered the family room and took the aisle, and I felt honored to be Greg's bride.

Colorful guests filled both sides of the room. As some grinned from ear to ear, others blotted tissue from wet eyes to wet cheeks and back again. Couples, both old and young, cuddled closely in the comfort of each other's arms. Hands held, feet caressed calves and lover's lips locked gently as they took full advantage of the moment. Indeed, love was in the air. While all the single *and* taken women *and* men in the crowd secretly fantasized over Greg, his eyes belonged to me. And while every other man, woman and child in the room focused on *me*, my eyes rested trustfully upon *him*. There wasn't a single place in the world that I would have rather been in that moment.

Greg's light gray tuxedo seemed to have been made just for him - a second soulmate, perhaps. The quality fabric enveloped his tight body as it catered to every muscular crease in his arms, chest, back and bottom. And with two two-hour gym visits every day for six months, there was no shortage of muscles. Muscles that I never thought I'd be as fond of as I grew to be. But that's a little too personal, isn't it?

As my beautiful cousin, Denise, stood and delivered a robust run in front of a fairy tale floral arch, a grand piano, and her pianist, my generous friend, Faith from college, played nearby. Four tearful bridesmaids and my best friend and emotional maid of honor, Gina, posed off-center behind her. It was even more beautiful than I could have ever dreamed or planned for, and I felt grateful to share that moment with those who meant the most to me.

Four dapper groomsmen and Greg's baby brother, my goofball soon-to-be brother-in-law, Nate, stood to their right. Their emotional mother, the sweet but straight-up, Ms. Evelyn, smiled as she sat alone in the front row. And Greg, the love of my life, stood tall, dark and confident. He gently clasped his strong hands below his waist as he relaxed his shoulders and patiently waited for me.

I closed my eyes and accepted my father's kiss on my forehead as he and I arrived at the altar. Gina and I made eye contact as he released me, and we shared our signature floating fist pump - a greeting that we made up back in fifth grade to show Michelle Robinson and Tangie Edwards that we were better off without them in the group anyway. Though it wasn't very creative, it was ours and it was a symbol of our unbreakable bond with one another. I love Gina so much and my memory of that special day makes me miss everything that we used to be and everything I hope to someday return to.

I nervously caressed my collarbone and felt my face blush as Greg undressed me with his beautiful brown eyes. The combination of those long lashes that boys tend to steal from their mothers and that captivating gaze made me think of the particular brand of Dutch dark cocoa that my mother uses in her brownies. Rich, smooth and inviting. Speaking of my mother, I caught a glimpse of her on the front pew, overcome with emotion. She sobbed, smiled and sighed simultaneously, and as she struggled to hold herself together, my loving father held her in his arms, like he did whenever he sensed she needed him to.

"Aww, mom," I mouthed as I held back more than a few tears of my own.

As Denise finished up her solo and headed to her seat, Reverend Daniels, the sweaty, robust, heavyset preacher from my parents' church, stood and greeted us in that loud and animated way that only Reverend Daniels could.

"Alright now! Love is up in this house today!" he proclaimed as he feverishly waved one hand in the air while gripping his bedazzled microphone with the other. "Can you feel it?!"

The crowd went wild, and I have to admit, so did I. I had not been to church in a number of years, but Reverend Daniels' energy reminded me of a much simpler time. A time when my worries consisted of choosing a pink or purple binder for school or which lip gloss paired better with my velour tracksuit - the glitter or the rainbow. It was a time when my responsibilities were few and the innocence of my youth was taken for granted. Rest in peace to those days, right?

"Ah, come on now!" Reverend Daniels belted out. "Can y'all *feel* the love up in this house?!"

"I do!" I prematurely announced as I found myself engulfed in the moment.

Yeah, the audience found that pretty funny.

"Slow your roll there, Miss Lauren," said Reverend Daniels. "There will be plenty of time for that."

I could hear Greg snickering as I bashfully covered my face with my hand.

"Sorry," I said.

"There ain't nothin' wrong with a woman who knows who she wants," Reverend Daniels defended, "and to be standing across from him, knowing that who she wants, wants her back... Amen! If that ain't a blessing!"

"Amen," Ms. Evelyn agreed as she smiled and nodded her head at me.

Ms. Evelyn is an exceptional woman, and I always felt fortunate to know her, long before Greg asked me to marry him. She has a kind yet straightforward way of delivering the truth to you that leaves you feeling inspired rather than torn apart. I have found that some people present as either one or the other. They destroy you with the depths of a truth you may not have even asked for, *or* they inspire you with dreams you may or may not possess the mental or physical capacity to handle. Ms. Evelyn, on the other hand, handed you the truth from a place of love and gifted dreams to those that needed them most because she sensed untapped talents that needed recognition. I like that about her.

She raised two Black boys independently while working a full-time and a part-time job. She did french rolls and finger waves out of her basement and faithfully led the Junior Usher Board at her church every second and fourth Sunday of the month. Greg and Nate never wanted for anything and Ms. Evelyn made sure of that. She also ensured that Greg grew into an incredible man, and Reverend Daniels was right... Standing across from the man of my dreams, knowing deep in my soul that I was the woman of *his,* was nothing shy of a blessing.

You know, I had the honor of growing up with two parents who were madly in love with each other, so from a very tender age, I *knew* love. Our home wasn't always filled with artificial grins and agreements either; sometimes, my parents fought. And they were careful not to hide it from me because they wanted me to understand that while true love isn't clear of complications, it is full of circumstances that oftentimes need to be worked out, adjustments that need to be made, and conversations that need to take place in order to get to whatever level is next in line. What remained consistent, though, was respect, integrity and a constant understanding that regardless of the bullshit that passes by, we're in this together. And while sometimes my mother and father would end the day angry with one another, that anger somehow managed to die off in the middle of the night.

Greg and I held hands and locked eyes as Reverend Daniels doted over our diamonds.

"Lord, have mercy!" he shouted as he closely examined the

rings. Our guests found that pretty funny, too.

And believe it or not, although I imagine by now that you will, I wound up wearing the same emerald cut diamond ring that I clipped from *Brides* back in nineteen ninety… never mind. You get the point. And I could not wait to finally wear it on my finger! Greg wasn't very knowledgeable about rings, so he didn't have much of a preference. So, we kept it versatile for him in that it was casual enough not to distract from a fun night out with the guys but still classy enough to "stunt on these hoes," as Greg so elegantly emphasized to the jeweler.

"We have all gathered here today to witness a celebration of love," Reverend Daniels proclaimed. "The very thing that brought Lauren and Greg into this world. And the very thing that will bind them together until life is no longer a thing. True love is incredible that way. Amen?"

The crowd agreed.

"Amen," he said. "The way it catches hold of you, swallows you whole and locks the door on everything that stands in its way. True love. Amen."

I could tell by the smirk on his face that Greg was holding in his laughter. Hell, I was holding mine in, too. And it was clear that Reverend Daniels was… well… feeling himself, just like I remember him doing every Sunday growing up. But just like then, we smiled and let him have his moment because no matter how precise the planning, these instances are simply unpredictable and made memories that could never be duplicated.

And soon, the time had come for us to exchange vows and rings. Greg gently wiped the tears from my eyes. The relaxing scent of Ylang Ylang made me smile as his Tiger's Eye essential oil bracelet gently grazed across my nose. I love that about him

- the way he cares for me, always needing to know that I am doing just fine. And back then, I liked to believe that I always was. Just fine. Now, I'm not so confident, though I do wish that I were.

"Do you, Gregory take Lauren to be your wife and partner in life?" Reverend Daniels asked, "to have and to hold from this day forward, for better or for worse, for richer or for poorer, in sickness and in health, to love and to cherish, till death do you part, according to Universal law, in the presence of love?"

Greg did. And so did I. My heart melted as he tenderly kissed both of my hands, tears of joy rolling down his soft, brown cheeks because he and I both knew that we both meant every word we agreed to.

"Now then, by the power vested in me by the Creator and by the sweet State of Georgia," he said, "I now pronounce you husband and wife! Gregory, you may now kiss your bride!"

Our home exploded with excitement as guests cheered us on from every corner of the room. The smiles were plentiful; the happiness - heartfelt and true. And as Greg and I shared a very French kiss, Denise sealed our deal with another romantic number - an original piece from her EP. Two ushers in white dramatically dragged open the double wooden doors —my mother's idea— while Greg and I jumped over an old wooden broom —his mother's idea— and happily strolled down the aisle toward them. The guests stood, clapped and moved to the music as we began the next chapter of our lives together. But first, a celebration was in order, and outfit number two —a retro romper I found hiding between the racks at one of my favorite vintage shops in town— was awaiting my arrival.

3

The Celebration

Servers strolled the yard with trays of cocktails and crab cakes in hand while a bartender entertained all of the singles. Tangelo and ivory linens alternately draped circular tables all around the yard, and pieces of vibrantly citrus floral arrangements with golden accents centered each one. Orange here. Yellow there. Gold everywhere! It was absolutely divine, and I would be far from the truth if I claimed a mere ounce of surprise.

Lauren has always been quite sure of herself. That's one thing I know! Even as an adolescent, she knew exactly what she wanted, how she wanted it to look and feel, and if she committed to it, well then, it was as good as done. As a matter of fact, when my obstetrician, Dr. Ruth Franklin - you know, the one with the private office with the stunning views on uh… Oh darn it, I forget the name of that street, but it's right off of Peachtree, behind that bank. It's been many moons since I was a patient there, but I think it's still standing. Anyway, when the doctor estimated my due date, Lauren was sure to arrive in a timely fashion, with a head full of curls and a strong voice full of certainty! Yep, that's my girl! Always been that way, my Lauren. That was, of course, until… Oh, never mind that. Where was I? Oh, that's right… The celebration!

I sat fairly central, so I had the great pleasure of seeing and hearing nearly everything that evening. A lazy lake served as a backdrop of sorts for a single dockside table with an ivory cloth draped over it that read "Mr. and Mrs". It was typed in an elegantly scripted font while a sleepy sun sat in the distance behind it. *Very* romantic, if I may add. Truth be told, I couldn't have made better selections myself.

Gregory's good friend, Roderick, the DJ, spun throwbacks, or whatever the young people were calling them back then. Guests sipped sangria and soda, fingers snapped, old ladies laughed and carefree cougars moved their bodies rhythmically to the beat. I swayed, bobbed my head and mingled as I saw fit.

Kenneth and I were sampling from a tray of hors d'oeuvres when I heard a rather loud screeching sound slapping against the microphone. It was none other than Gregory's brother, Nathan, Evelyn's youngest son. I think that most would describe him as slender, debatably attractive and somewhat of a class clown. And I think he surprised us all when he stepped onto the dock and, with a half-empty glass of wine in one hand, grabbed the microphone with the other and delivered a… well, a speech.

"Yo… Pardon me. Hey, hey, hey, everybody! May I have your attention for a moment?" he asked, or however he phrased it.

Please, don't quote me on that. It's, rather, out of my way. It's quite funny when I think back on that moment. Those who weren't familiar with the goofy young man looked all around - some concerned for their safety, others concerned for *his*.

"Please?" he begged. "I won't keep y'all. I promise."

Again, don't quote me.

Guests gossiped as all eyes in the yard cautiously turned to him and the very doubtful DJ lowered the music. And nearby, I eavesdropped as Evelyn struck conversation with a curious middle-aged woman.

"Evelyn isn't that…That's Nathan?!" she queried as she squinted her eyes and leaned forward for confirmation. "I thought that was your boy! Help him, Jesus."

"Girl, that's the trouble we in," I heard sweet Evelyn say as she and the woman shared a chuckle. "I don't think nobody's listening."

I have to admit, though, I am awfully fond of Evelyn. Lauren wasn't a difficult child, not in the least. However, I cannot even begin to imagine what it must have been like to raise two young boys all on my own. Sure, Nathan is a bit of a buffoon, but he's a very decent young man. And Gregory, well… sometimes it seems like he was created and raised *just* for my Lauren. Even if I focused on it, I don't believe I could ever see her with another man. And Evelyn, while she is a bit more "around the way" than the other women in my circle, I think she's quite lovely. I really do.

"Nathan?!" Evelyn loudly whispered as she folded her arms and narrowed her eyes.

"What, ma?" Nathan answered as if he felt like he'd outgrown his mother's grip. "Why you whispering like that?" he asked.

Oh, dear God. The thought of that moment still brings me so much laughter. And poor Evelyn, he nearly gave her a heart attack!

"Boy, quit fooling around," she told him. "And get down before you fall in that water!" she shouted. "Child, that boy can't swim," she told the woman next to her.

"Everything is under control," he respectfully assured her. "I'm not gonna mess this up, Mama."

Still not completely convinced, Evelyn pressed her lips together as she pushed back into her seat. With all eyes on her, she looked around the yard, shook her head from side to side and released an enormous sigh.

"Lord, help me," she said.

Nathan took a deep breath and a sip from his glass, cleared his throat and began with a soft smile.

"Okay, okay. Here we go," he said. "Alright, so listen y'all, I know this ain't the right time for speeches or whatnot, but this ain't really a speech. It's… more of a… Okay, it's a speech."

As you can imagine, that broke the ice.

"This is harder than I thought it would be," he confessed.

"Take your time, Nate!" one of the groomsmen in the back blurted out as the young man grew emotional, which I thought was incredibly kind of him.

"My brother don't know this," Nathan continued. "But after he asked me to be his best man, I cried. The whole way home. I just kept asking myself… *How?* How can I be *his* best man when he's the best man I've ever known?"

That last bit brought tears to my eyes, not that they were all that far from the surface anyway. By that point, Nathan had definitely earned our attention. And I tried hard not to give in to my peripheral, but I simply could not help myself. I turned and watched through the window as Gregory, who was observing from the kitchen of the house, listened as his baby brother spoke in a way that he clearly had not heard him speak before. After a few seconds, Lauren joined him and I quickly shifted my eyes back to Nathan.

"I was so young when our pops passed away," Nathan said,

"I sometimes have a hard time remembering him. I mean, I know he was there, but I struggle to remember what having him around *felt* like, you know? The realness of it. Y'all know what I'm trying to say. My mother always did her best to help me remember and to make sure I knew that I was loved," he said after he took a moment to gather himself, "and every day, I'm thankful for that."

Evelyn secured a tissue from her purse; it didn't take a mathematician to figure out what that was for.

"But Greg—" his voice cracked, "damn. He ain't just a good brother, y'all. He was all I ever needed. Still is."

Nathan laughed at himself as he cleared his throat. And I promise you, I did not intend to pry, but when I just happened to turn that way, I noticed that Lauren was wiping Gregory's eyes with a napkin. Oh, I lost it at that very moment. How incredibly sweet! See, this is why I'm not fond of weddings. I mean, I am. But I always leave them in such a wreck!

"Alright, that's enough of that," Nathan continued. "Everybody, please turn around and join me in welcoming the newest, flyest married couple on the block… My big bro and his fine boo thang, *the* Mr. and Mrs. Gregory Winters! Come on, y'all, give it up for 'em! They deserve it!"

And truly, I do not speak this way regularly, so forgive me if I sound rather clunky. I am just doing my best to recall the events from that day, that's all. So, please accept this as an indefinite disclaimer as we move forward. Thank you.

Suddenly, the crowd went bonkers as the beaming lovebirds exited the back patio door of the house and joined us in the lavish yard, hand in hand. We've never spoken about the instance, but judging by Evelyn's ear-to-ear smile, I believe that Nathan had surpassed her expectations. He undoubtedly surpassed mine.

I ruined every dash of my makeup that evening, but, in my opinion, it was well worth it. And I sure am grateful to have had my Kenneth right by my side for comfort, as always. Lord knows I needed it. We all did. And we all still do.

* * *

I was really just there to support my girl, Lauren, so I wouldn't say that I was watching Nathan like that or anything, but yes, I did notice him. I thought he was kinda cute but just super silly. He wasn't really my type, but yeah… I saw him. What he said about Greg, I thought it was sweet. I had never heard a man talk about another man that way, so I guess it kinda made me look at him differently. Not that I was looking. I heard him. That's what I'm trying to tell you. I *heard* him. There's a difference.

Now, the wedding… that was beautiful! Lauren *always* had great taste! My homegirl used to win every fashion show in school, all the girls wanted to be her and all the boys wanted to be with her. But she didn't have time for that! She was focused. Driven. And damn, she *always* had a way with that pen, even when she *claimed* that she wanted to be a doctor! Of course, I supported her. That's my girl. But I already knew that wasn't her calling.

I remember back in seventh grade when Mr. Cartwright had given us this writing assignment. We had just two weeks to write fifteen pages on the people of whatever African country we chose. Now at the time, I hated writing! I'm cool with it now, but back then, I was a much better speaker. All of my teachers knew, assign Gina a speech, and she is gon' kill it!

Writing was a different story. But in just three days, Lauren turned in the most jaw-dropping thirty-one-page essay any of us had ever read before. She got an A+ on that paper and Mr. Cartwright was so impressed that he assigned the rest of us Lauren's paper! We had to read it and write *another* essay on what *she* wrote. It was *that* good, y'all! For real.

So, the type of success that Lauren has had with her writing career, I'm not shocked. It's been inside of her. She just needed the right people to believe in her as much as she believed in herself. Once that happened, it was a wrap. I mean, look at the house they bought! Don't get me wrong, Greg is successful, too. They both are. But you know, I'm *Lauren's* ride-or-die. And even though this bullshit happened to her, I still love her and I'll be right here whenever she's ready to talk.

But that wedding night, it was perfect y'all. After Nathan gave his speech, the DJ crunk up the music and Lauren and Greg looked so damned good as they joined the rest of us in the backyard. No doubt, everybody loved them. And I saw Nathan looking at me, but I turned right back around, got myself another drink and pretended not to notice. But I noticed. I was there by myself, you know. I was single at the time and I really didn't have anybody to invite, so I just showed up.

Lauren looked amazing! Her and Greg was doing all of that little cute shit, too. She smiled, leaned into Greg, he smiled back. Then he pulled her hand up to his lips and kissed it, flexing his double dimples. *All* the cute shit! You hear me? And I ain't gon' lie, Lauren did alright for herself. Greg is a good-looking man, he loves her and he shows her every day. That's all I ever wanted for her.

The party lasted for a lil' minute; you know how we do. It

got dark, crickets started doing their thing and we just kept having a good time. Folks was stuffed, too! Damn gluttons, belching all loud and shit, lying to themselves, talking about "this my last bite," knowing good and well that it wasn't true. But I had to stop eating because if I didn't, my ass was gon' pop right up out of that dress! Talk about embarrassing!

I made my way over to Lauren's parents' table, Mr. and Mrs. Ellis - they're pretty much my family. So, I'm sitting there, right? Tell me why PawPaw… My bad, that's Lauren's granddaddy. Tell me why this dude pushed his chair away from the table, reached into his navy blue Dickies style shirt pocket and pulled out a toothpick?! Like, what the fuck, PawPaw? This shit is way too fancy for all of that. This dude started sucking his teeth with his tongue then he proceeded to *scrub* them! Oh, my God, y'all!

Mrs. Ellis noticed him, right? So, of course, she yelled at him.

"Dad?! Put that toothpick away!" she said as she clenched her teeth.

But he just rolled his eyes away from her.

"Now, please!" she halfway asked when he clearly didn't listen.

And you could tell she was getting a little embarrassed because she looked around at everybody, smiled and started fluffing her hair. I thought it was over, but then PawPaw slapped the table, turned around and started talking to Mr. Ellis.

"Kenny, come on!" he said. "Every goddamn time I go somewhere with y'all, somebody wanna tell me what to do. I don' had enough! I'm 77 years old, you know."

No, he wasn't, y'all.

"Dad, you're 87, not 77," Mrs. Ellis chimed in before PawPaw really flipped the fuck out.

"Hell, I'm a grown-ass man!" he proclaimed. "Hear me? Somebody betta tell her! I'm *her* daddy, goddamn it! I know how old I am. Shit!"

I was sitting there shook! I have been to my fair share of Ellis family events, but this wedding topped every last one of them. And Mr. Ellis tried to calm PawPaw down, but he wasn't having it. Nope.

"Y'all is just full of shit! Both of y'all!" he said as he fixed his suspenders, puffed his chest out and stormed off.

Y'all, I was cryin'! I was about to go catch up with Lauren, but I saw her and Greg kickin' it at that table on the dock. That shit was *so* nice. I was so happy for both of them. I love my best friend and I *love* Black love. I just never expected shit to go down like it did, you know? None of us did, really.

* * *

I knew she would be mad at me, but that food was delicious. It should have been, as much as it cost us. But whatever my baby wanted, she got. No questions asked. If you asked me, though, I would have been just fine getting married at the courthouse but Lauren had a vision and I felt responsible for helping her execute it. I can't even lie, it turned out amazing and Lauren looked more beautiful than I even knew she could.

She looked so damn edible sitting there next to me, smiling as she looked out at our family and friends. She was happy as hell. Full of joy. And my fat ass had to go and ruin the moment! She acted like I *tried* to burp, though. Nah, it wasn't even like that.

"Babe?! Really?" she asked as her smile ended real fast.

"What?" I replied as I raised my eyebrows and acted like I didn't know what she was talking about.

"Don't *what* me," she said. "You're full!"

"Just a little bit," I told her.

Okay, it was a lot of bit, and she knew it. She jabbed my arm so hard. It hurts just thinking about it.

"Just a little bit?" she asked. "You promised me! You know you can't stay awake when you're full. It's our wedding night, Greg! You're going to eat away all of your muscles!" she added.

So, I did what I do when I've made her mad and I'm trying to fix it. You know what I mean? I grinned, wrapped my arms around her and gently kissed her on the side of her neck. She liked it, too.

"Baby, I tried not to," I said, "but then I had some of that steak with the sauce and then the cheesecake…."

I had her then.

"I can't stand you. You are a mess!" she exclaimed as she started laughing.

I kissed her again and her smile came back to me. Damn, I miss that smile.

"I know," I told her, "but I'm your mess."

She bit that bottom lip, I slid my hand up her thigh, and, not to be too explicit, but she already knew what time it was.

"All mine. And you know what?" she asked.

"What's that?" I replied.

She pulled back, and man, I thought we was about to get it cracking right there in front of everybody. I've never been that type of guy, but that's only because it's never happened before. But man, Lauren was really mad.

"Your messy ass better not be doing all this kissing and

rubbing and then fall asleep as soon as we get upstairs!!" she *told* my ass.

But I just laughed and let her know what it was. "I'm all yours tonight, Mrs. Winters."

"That sounds good, huh?" she smiled and said. "Mrs. Winters."

She liked hearing that.

I licked my lips, and I kid you not, your boy was ready for a whole new party. She knew it, too.

"You are so nasty, *Mr. Winters,*" she said.

We got back to kissing, and just when I thought I couldn't take it no more, them damn metal spoons started hitting glasses. Lauren laughed as she moved her soft lips off mine and turned to face everybody. Then she wiped her lipstick from my lips with her thumb. She always used to take care of me like that.

"Come on, baby. Time to mingle," she said as she grabbed my hand and stood to her feet. But based on my, um… my situation, I wasn't all that ready to stand up. I mean, I was standing, but… you know what I'm saying?

4

The Consolidation

The celebration was in full swing, and as the night went on and we all became more acquainted with one another, it started to feel like more of a good old-fashioned gathering... a consolidation of our families, if you will. It was precious; it really was. Music moved the yard as guests filled the dance floor. Some bobbed their heads —myself included— some pop-locked, some simply tapped their feet, and others huddled as they hustled to songs from eras both familiar and unfamiliar to me. Nevertheless, we had a fine time!

My father and his country shenanigans were getting on all of my nerves simultaneously, but I sure did love to see him and Lauren dance together. Lauren was always such a carefree dancer. She wasn't one for choreographed moves, but she could definitely cut a rug of her own. But my father, well, he and my mother met at a dance competition back in their day. They were opponents, but they fell head over heels in love with one another at the end of their forty-eight-hour shindig when they were the only two people left standing on their feet. By the time I was born, their dancing had mostly ended, but there are numerous photographs that validate their claims of fame in various dance circuits around the Southeast.

"Bet you didn't know old PawPaw could still get down, did you?" my father asked Lauren as she struggled to keep up with him.

"PawPaw, just what do you call this move?" she asked.

My father twisted and turned until he landed in some sort of Charley-horse position.

"Used to call this The Moose," he replied.

Lauren burst into laughter, as did I.

"The moose?!" Lauren asked.

"Come on, let me show you how to do it," he insisted.

As the two of them laughed and enjoyed one another, I was reminded just how precious life is and that sometimes, it sneaks away when you least expect it. Some days, that thought brings me great comfort. Others, not so much.

* * *

Anybody who knows me knows that I love my boys more than anything in the whole world. That's a fact! And I know they're both grown now with their own lives, but when I look at them, all I see is my babies. My handsome little boys! Greg, with all that confidence he had and dreams that I couldn't always wrap my head around… and Nate, just trotting behind him, trying to keep up with him cause Greg was real cool, you know. Them boys was a mess!

Goodness gracious, I didn't know what I was gon' do when Harvey died and left me alone to care for 'em. I remember that day like it just happened, and seem like every time I try *not* to think about it, I just can't help myself. I had gone grocery shopping down at that market that used to be off of Reed Road. You know the one I'm talkin' 'bout? The one where Terry Wright used to be the manager? Beverly's boy? You probably wasn't born yet, was you? Anyway, I was almost home, then I turned around and went back because I forgot to pick up some pecans for my pies. Harvey loved his pecan pies, boy, I tell you. He would sit there and swallow them pies whole if you let 'em!

So, when I finally got back home, I found my husband laid out in the bed, just where I had left him that morning. The boys was sitting out there in the living room in their pajamas, watching their cartoons. I went over to Harvey and tried to wake him up after he didn't answer me, but he wouldn't move. Po' Harvey had died in his sleep. Doctor said his heart just quit working, and I near 'bout ended up in somebody's psych ward 'cause a piece of my heart had gone with him and I didn't think I could carry on.

Greg was eight when his daddy passed away, but Nate wasn't old enough to really know what was going on. All he knew was that his daddy wasn't around no mo', and sooner than later, Harvey left his mind altogether. I would pull out my picture albums and do my best to remind him about his daddy, but I think he was just too little and too young to understand back then. It was tough, those days. But God kept us, like he always has. And my, look how far he's brought all of us.

It's a shame, you know, what happened to Lauren. Bless her heart. But I believe she'll come back around in her own way and in her own time. Just got to be patient. I enjoyed the wedding, though. I did. Nobody can't ever say that Lauren don't have good taste either, 'cause that's a lie! That girl and her mama, whew, Jesus! Them women can dress and they know just about *every* color there is to know. First and last time I ever heard of YInMn Blue was when Lauren told me it was one of her favorite colors and that she was thinking of layering it in her living room. Hell, I just smiled and listened to her talk about it but I really couldn't make out nothin' she was sayin'. All I knew about was the regular blues and the ones you get when your heart been messed with. Never heard nothin' 'bout no YInMn Blue! It is pretty, though.

Now, that reception was a sight to see! *Gorgeous!* Just gorgeous. And I don't know who smothered them turkey wings but Lord, Jesus! They put they foot in them turkey wings! I think I dozed off for a couple of minutes after I ate, too, but I didn't wanna leave my boy's wedding celebration without dancing just a lil' bit. Now, I used to dance all the time when I was a young woman, but I do recall Greg trying to teach me something or other, like I was starting from scratch.

"Ma, you gotta slide," he told me. "You can't be over here doing this old corporate waltz," he said. "It's not even that type of music, mama."

That boy sure knows how to make me laugh. He also knows how to get on my damn nerves.

"Boy, hush," I fussed. "Dancing is how *you* got here, you know. You and your brother."

That shut him up!

"Gross, ma! You just nasty," he said as we made our way right on off of that dance floor.

"You nasty too," I told him. "Don't think I didn't see you over there playing house at that table."

I know he didn't think I saw him, but when I told him when he was a little bitty boy that I see it all, I meant I see it all! Now, of course, that made him turn all red about the face, but

I thought it was funny. Boy never could get away with doing nothin' he didn't have no business doin'!

Then Nate wobbled his goofy ass on over there.

Talkin' 'bout, "What y'all laughin' at?"

Then he took off just as quick as he came when he saw Gina over there at that bar sitting by herself.

"That boy stay chasing ass!" I told Greg.

"Ma?" he replied in shock.

He knew I was right.

"You're not supposed to say *ass*," he said.

Child, I clenched my teeth and swung my purse into his arm with all my might.

"Quit cussin', boy!" I told him. "That's not how I raised you. Now, you know better!"

He wiggled and waned, and of course, my old school whippin' won in the end. Lord knows, I had gotten too old to be carrying on like that, but I love Greg, I do. And it just ain't fair what happened, you know. It just ain't right.

* * *

I was just sitting at the bar, minding my own business. Moving my head to the beat, sipping my cranberry and… I know it wasn't vodka because me and vodka don't mix all that well, but it was something. But anyway, Nathan pulled up an empty bar stool and sat right next to me. He licked his lips and gave it his best shot or whatever you wanna call it.

"Well, damn! I hope you catch the bouquet!" he said like he had been practicing what to say to me and had convinced himself that *that* was the way to go.

"We can get married and start making babies tonight!" he

continued.

He clearly didn't know that it was a little too late for me to catch the bouquet, but I was curious about how hard he'd try, so I entertained him.

"Excuse me?" I asked.

"I saw you checking me out," he said. "At the engagement party. The altar. After my speech…."

"*This* dude," I thought to myself.

"You did *not* see me checking you out," I contended.

"Bam! See? I knew it!" he exclaimed as he clapped his hands all loud and shit.

"Knew what?" I replied.

"You *were* checkin' me out," he said. "Old slick ass."

"I did not say I was checking you out," I maintained in an effort to hold my ground.

"Nah, you said I didn't *see* you checkin' me out," he said. "There's a difference."

I will admit, he did make me laugh.

"I'm on to you, girl," he said with that half smile, showing off that one dimple.

He *is* funny, but I'm a lady, so I wasn't giving in *that* easily.

"Wow. You just don't give up, do you?" I asked.

"Nope," he said as we shared a laugh.

"So, how'd you end up being the maid of honor anyway?" he asked.

I told him how Lauren and I had been friends since preschool, and he told me a joke that I honestly don't remember, but, knowing Nathan, I'm sure it was funny.

* * *

I knew that Gregory was the one for Lauren even before she knew he was. I think that as fathers, we never want to give our daughters away to any man because some just aren't fit for the young women we're raising. But when Gregory came into the picture, he was just so easy to love from the start. That young man, he had more manners than me, he came from a good family, he had a vision for his life that included my daughter and he had such a strong work ethic, you know what I mean? And now, I don't swing that way, but Gregory is a handsome fella. Sure, he is. He was just the whole package, and I knew it was only a matter of time before Lauren felt like she wouldn't be able to manage without him. After a while, all she did was talk about "Greg this" or "Greg that". That's when I knew he was special to her and I couldn't have been happier for her. Lauren and I always had a special connection, and I'd like to believe that we still do because it makes me feel better about the whole ordeal.

I'll never forget that wedding celebration. Boy, it was something! Lauren looked real pretty, just like her mother did the day we got married. We all enjoyed being in one another's company, and after a while, it just felt like we were one big old happy family. It started getting pretty late, and I figured Robin would be ready to turn in soon, but I couldn't let the night end without having a good old-fashioned sit down with Gregory. Man to man, you know?

"I'm just really, really proud of you, young man," I told him as we sat and watched over the party. "The way you love my daughter and the way you two come together to make this thing work… It's impressive. I mean, it really is," I told him.

"Thank you, sir. I appreciate that," he replied in that humble yet confident Gregory-style.

He reminds me of myself, in a way - that drive and that resilience. Mmhmm.

"No, no, no, no, no," I said to him. "No more of that *sir* stuff, you hear me?" I confirmed. "I've gained a son, alright? From here on out, you call me "Pops"."

Same thing I called my father, and the same thing my father told Robin she could call him, but she just insisted on calling him Mr. Ken because she believed in putting handles on your name if you were of a certain age. I'm a little more casual, myself. But, that's Robin.

"And anything you need," I continued on with Gregory, "I'm here for you. Understand?"

He grinned and looked at me like… I don't know… like he trusted me, you know?

"I do," he said. "And that means a lot to me."

I knew it did. He had lost his daddy when he was just a little boy, you know. It's a shame. It really is, but as long as I was around, I wanted him to know that he could count on me if he ever needed anything. And that ain't never changed. Sometimes men just need other men to talk about men things with, you know? Robin says the same thing about women, but I've never been one, so I can't say. I just take her word for it.

"Now…tell me all about this big old house you got my baby living in," I joked.

Well, not really, because I wanted to know. There I was, telling him to call me anytime he needed *me*, but from the looks of it, he had everything covered. House could fit two more houses inside of it; it was just that big! Lauren told me how much that house set 'em back and I almost spit my coffee out! I sure was proud, though.

Things aren't what they used to be, you know? I just hope

that Lauren can sort this thing out and they can move on with their lives together. It's just not right.

* * *

I never did keep many women friends around, but I like Robin. She's a little prissy, but she's got a good heart on her. We have good talks, she and I, and I'll say it again: the woman sure can dress. That's the truth! So, she knew exactly where I was coming from.

"Whew, yes, honey!" I told her. "I'm just glad they gave me a couple of options because that first dress had me looking like a damned Jolly Rancher!"

She just 'bout fell over laughing!

"What flavor?" she asked.

"Watermelon, hell!" I told her.

"You should've seen mine," she said with her hand sticking out like this here. "The color was fantastic, but that style... oh no!" she said. "Sucked all of my hips in, girl, and that's my best feature!"

Yeah, I like Robin. She's funny, too. But she's a mother first, so our relationship is a little different. We might have different stories about how we got to this place, but me and Robin, in more ways than you might think, we the same.

We was talkin' and I had to tell her, "I'm just so happy to have Lauren join my family." She's like the daughter I never had."

I knew she understood what I meant.

"Evelyn, Kenneth and I couldn't ask for a better husband for Lauren," she said as she grabbed 'hold of my hand. "I'm so happy that they found one another. I truly am," she continued.

I believed every word she said, too. Despite everything that happened, you know, I still do. Sometimes you have to hold on to your faith. Sometimes that's all you got left. That's what I'm doing, holding on. You understand what I'm telling you?

* * *

Now Greg might be cute and everything —and I'm only saying that because he's my brother— but in my opinion, one dimple is better than two. With this face, I can keep a woman surprised *and* excited. Look at all the faces I can make. That's cool, ain't it? Well, I think it is. Anyway, man, I knew I could snag Gina. I'm not trying to be funny but look at all of this! All it took was a little conversation that night and her hard-ass cover was blown.

She kept on telling me how crazy I was, but I just had to let her know, "This is me, Gina! I just, um… I guess I just always go for what I like".

That's what I told her when she asked me why I was moving so fast. But I liked what I saw, a lot. All that pretty hair, her smile and that as-… oh, I can't say that, can I? Oh, I can? Okay, well then, her ass.

We locked eyes for a minute, then she looked away again and started rubbing the back of her neck. So, I just cut right to the chase.

"So, um… Are you single or what?" I asked her."

"Oh, wow," she said. "Just get right to it, huh?"

And I do. I cut right to the chase. Greg taught me that much.

* * *

I had gotten rather tired, but I was really enjoying my chitchat with Evelyn. We swapped all sorts of stories, and I think we became good friends that night. You know, I can't recall at the moment exactly what we were discussing, but I do remember Lauren interrupting - all full of joy like she always was back then.

"My two favorite women in the whole wide world, laughing and having girl-talk, smiling and stylish," she said as she made her way over to us.

That girl could make anyone smile - myself included. Now, I'm certainly not much of a dancer, but that night when she grabbed my hand and spun me around, I felt like a little girl all over again. A little dizzy, too, but it was fun. Evelyn smiled as she watched us.

"So, what are you two ladies talking about?" Lauren inquired.

"Babies," Evelyn fibbed.

"I should've known," Lauren replied as she rolled her eyes to the back of her head.

We looked out at the dance floor and watched as Nathan and Gina slow-danced with one another.

"Looks like somebody's having a good time," I commented.

"He's been talking about that girl since the engagement party," Evelyn added.

"Well, I think they're cute," Lauren said as she smiled.

I suppose they were.

After a few moments, the crowd dispersed, the dance music faded and a beautiful ballad took its place. I'll never forget the look in Lauren's eyes when she looked over at me, because as grown-up as she'd become, all I saw was my little girl.

"Aww, mom, that's our song," she said, looking beautiful and radiant.

"Go on," I urged her as I saw Kenneth take the dance floor.

Evelyn and I smiled as my two loves reunited after such a long day, and shortly after, Gregory joined us as an onlooker.

"You know we want a girl, don't you?" Evelyn joked with him.

"I should have known," Gregory replied in the same tone as Lauren's.

I really do believe that those two are soulmates. But even soulmates lose their way sometimes, don't you think?

* * *

The day was no less than perfect. I was exhausted by the end of it, but there was no way that I wanted the night to be over. At least not without a dance with my first love.

"You know you're always going to be my baby girl, don't you?" my father reminded me in that soothing voice of his.

"I know. And you'll always be my daddy," I reassured him as he rocked me slowly in the comfort of his arms, his Old Spice masking every other scent at the party.

"Well, it's settled then," he said. "We'll always get on each other's damn nerve," he continued as we shared a laugh so sweet.

My father and I have always had those laughs. And I would give everything I've ever owned to feel as alive as I felt that night. But without change, who are we? With it, too, I suppose.

5

The Change

"The only way to ensure the accurate execution of anything is to do it yourself," my mother would always say.

And for most of my life, I subscribed to that ideology, especially with regard to my health, physical appearance, and ultimately, my career. For years, I worked my ass off trying to compete with a country full of creatives like myself. I practically begged publishers to get my books on the shelves, toning down my style to fit into spaces that were never designed to accommodate me. I had finally had enough of that shit, and I decided to publish my own books and distribute them in my own way. That's when the course of my career as a writer changed.

My books climbed the independent lists so quickly, I could barely keep my phone lines clear. One, after another, after another - all calling in effort to gain the upper hand on the next organizer, blogger, or whomever they were in competition with. They all shared the same motive: I was hot and they all wanted me for one thing or another.

Aside from owning my career, I owned who I was as an individual. I loved wearing my hair in its natural state, and I preferred to wear my coils free and cut into a particular shape that enhanced the features of my face rather than confining them to braids or twists that required more maintenance than I had the time or patience for. And I cared more about preserving my edges than slaying them, if you know what I mean. But after paying more ill-skilled cosmetologists than I was able to keep count of, I decided that the only way to get the 'do that I desired was to *do* it myself. Hell, I even mastered the manicure because chasing down Lee was exhausting, and equally embarrassing!

And maybe this is a bit more information than you bargained for, but why pay a stranger to rip hairs from your vagina when you can rip them off yourself? Well, not *your* vagina, per se… mine. That's always been my thought, and although I never minded spending money, I certainly *did* mind wasting it, and I wasn't willing to change that. Well, *pregnancy* forced me to accept some things that I simply could not change. And I found that very difficult to deal with. I also found it difficult to *see* my vagina after a while, so, there went that.

Another thing about pregnancy that I wasn't too fond of was the doctor telling me that I should avoid lifting heavy things. Now, unless I was at the gym, I never really had to lift anything heavy anyway, but there was something about taking orders that never did sit well with me. So, the day we received our baby's furniture was a lot less magical than I had fantasized it to be.

I popped my hip to one side, pressed my lips together and folded my arms over my big bump as I tried my hardest to distract myself with anything I could set my eyes on. I tried to focus on the nearly nude trees, the colorfully fallen leaves and the bright gray sky that encompassed the front yard. I even gave attention to our senile seventy-nine-year-old neighbor, Mrs. Banfield, who *thought* she was washing her car but had apparently forgotten to turn the water hose on. Despite my efforts to distract myself, I was very uncomfortable having to observe from the doorway as Greg guided the two delivery men from their truck to the house. I gasped and grabbed my chest as one of the men stumbled and nearly fell over my flowers! Luckily, Greg was there to catch his fall.

"Damn, you alright?" he asked. "Be careful, man."

"Got that right!" I thought to myself.

"It took me forever to find that crib and it was the last one at the store!" I yelled out as I tried really hard not to get involved, taking a long, deep breath as Greg and the stumbler neared the doorway.

"Baby, I got this, okay?" Greg assured me. "I just need you to go relax and wait until this is all over," he said. "Can you please just do that for me? Maybe you could make yourself a nice sandwich or take a nap or something. Huh?"

"Why, Greg? Because I'm fat as hell?!" I asked, offended.

"Baby, no. You're not fat," he said. "It's lunchtime. Or nap time. You decide," he kindly suggested.

No way I believed him. I hadn't been that chubby since I was an infant, and even then, my mother said that I was much slimmer than the other babies in our family. But at that moment, I wasn't sure who was more out of shape - me or the fat black cat slowly strolling down the sidewalk. As it stared at me with those stupidly squinted eyes, I glared back.

"Baby?" Greg called as his eyes followed mine, landing on the mysterious creature in passing. "Lauren, come on, baby," he begged. "Please just go in the house," he said, knowing good and well what I would do to that creepy ass motherfucker if it didn't result in jail time. "Leave that damn cat alone, alright?"

"Fine," I said as I rolled my eyes and turned the other way.

I did look back once more before going inside, though. You can never be too sure when it comes to those things.

That summer, I told Gina that I wanted her to help me overcome my feelings about cats, and of course, she agreed to help me however she could. I figured if I made the commitment, there was no way that I wouldn't hold up my end of the agreement. I wasn't a quitter and once I set my mind on a task, nothing could get in the way of me completing it. Well, needless to say, I'm still a work in progress.

People would always ask me if some sort of trauma was the source of my aversion to cats. And honestly, I'm not sure. For as long as I can remember, the mere sight of them caused me tremendous discomfort. Perhaps it's their nature of unpredictability. The way they fixate on you, honing in on the wires of your soul and knowing secrets you've yet to share with anyone, answers to questions you've yet to ask. Whatever the reason, I have but one bottom line: I hate cats, and if I had it my way, they wouldn't exist among us.

As I settled back inside the house, I remember there was this haunting hymn calling from upstairs. I cautiously approached the spiral staircase and slowly made my way from the bottom of the stairs to the top, navigating the long hallway toward the master like one of those white girls in a poorly produced horror flick. You know how they always run toward the direction of danger, then spend the remainder of the film wondering why they're being chased? Well, I *knew* no one was there, but in the back of my mind, I knew the possibility still existed. *Something* has to inspire those sorts of films, doesn't it?

Suddenly, a horrific scream hailed from *our* bedroom! I rushed in, only to find a woman in blue scrubs being dragged through the woods by a monster. Damn television! I further examined our otherwise perfectly peaceful bedroom and found our large wooden ceiling fan blowing quietly above our California King bed. I think I took that bed for granted.

Anyway, the thin, white curtains gently swayed from side to side to the rhythm of the wind. Our large bamboo plants sat in two corners of the room, and the erotically ethnic painting that Ms. Evelyn had gifted us back-dropped the bed. Everything was exactly how I had left it, which washed away any remaining worry that a killer was on the loose. You don't have to remind me that I watched way too many murder mystery shows back then. I have since learned my lesson. Mostly. Alright, fine... I haven't.

So, I turned the television off, slid out of my fuzzy slippers, laid down on the bed and quickly drifted off to sleep. And almost immediately upon the commencement of my dream, a wild wind swept through the room, papers flew all about, objects fell and my serenity abruptly ended as I hopped up and quickly scanned the room for an explanation. The culprit? An open window and a wind advisory that I had apparently overlooked earlier in the day. As I shut the window and tidied our bedroom, I started to feel like a nap was no longer in the cards. And surprisingly, I wasn't very hungry.

"Maybe I'll make myself useful and do some writing," I thought.

Midday naps were never quite my thing anyway, so when my doctor told me to take things easy, well, I took that as more of an *opinion* rather than an order. She had given enough orders, anyway. But writing never required much effort, even if I had made a successful career out of it.

I am a lifelong storyteller so becoming an author was more of a natural progression than a purposeful pursuit. I only toyed around with the idea of becoming a neurosurgeon because I was doing research for a school paper, and I stumbled across an incredibly inspiring article about a young, Black neurosurgeon who had separated and then adopted a set of conjoined Cameroonian twins. I remember thinking how noble of an act that was and how big of heart it must have required, and I soon found myself sitting across from my guidance counselor reviewing required courses and prerequisites that I clearly hadn't met. But unless the balance in my bank account was in question, I wasn't all that interested in math, or science, for that matter. So, I retreated to the thing that brought me the most joy in life: my writing.

* * *

Family-filled frames, a billion bookcases, eccentric paintings and dual diplomas set the scene for my creative sanctuary, as I liked to call it. As I entered my office and pulled out my luxurious leather chair, I took a seat and reviewed notes I'd written on a pad atop my vintage glass desk. I had been working on a new novel —a psychological thriller— and I had been torn between two potential pathways for the protagonist. She would either remain a prisoner of her own parallel universe and succumb to the comforts of mediocrity, *or* she would venture out into the unknown to discover the true depth of her dreams.

As I closed my eyes and pondered which perspective was best for her, I could hear Greg instructing the delivery men in the near distance. *Something* crashed, and it took gaining control of every muscle in my body for me not to hop out of that chair, fly down those stairs and deliver the damn furniture myself! But as I spun around in my seat, I caressed my belly and flinched as a sharp stabbing pain in my lower abdomen suddenly caught me completely off-guard. Within a matter of seconds, I went from feeling familiar fetal pokes and twirls to struggling to breathe through what had taken over my body, forcing me to surrender to its power. As I pulled myself out of the chair and ultimately took hold of the arm of the sofa across from me, I lost my balance and collapsed, thankfully, into the cushions.

As I laid there, panting, groaning and crying my heart out - squealing Greg's name, hoping to be heard while also hoping that the worst was a mere figment of my imagination, I couldn't help but wonder if the due date I had been given had been inaccurately calculated. I was only six months along, anyway. Surely, the excruciating pain in my pelvis was just a simple side effect of being with child. That's what I thought, anyway. Or hoped. But either way, I was wrong. I was very, *very* wrong.

Perhaps it was the stress of the situation, or maybe she had simply developed as much as she was willing to. Whatever the reasoning behind it, *it was time,* and I was only a few unbearable contractions away from being certain. As Greg rushed me into the Emergency Room, I just remember feeling very overwhelmed with everything. Of course, I had read a multitude of books and articles on miscarriages, stillbirths and early infant losses, but I just assumed that those sorts of things only happened to women who didn't look after themselves.

And I did; I looked after myself! I maintained a healthy diet, I exercised religiously and I always took my prenatal vitamins.

So, even though I knew these misfortunes were possibilities, neither of them was a possibility that I was willing to accept. But I felt flooded with an array of emotions that I couldn't identify at the moment because I wasn't really sure what we were dealing with, but I knew the outcome was out of my hands.

When I look back on that time in my life, I feel so foolish.

"Why didn't I know?" I still ask myself.

As aware of my body as I had always been, why in the hell wasn't I aware that I was losing my baby? May I have a moment, please?

Greg and I had planned for her arrival from the day we found out that I was pregnant, and I had always dreamed of being a mother. As an only child, I kept more imaginary friends than I'm confident enough to confess. Sure, I had cousins —Denise being my favorite— and of course, I had Gina. But I never wanted our playtime to end because I didn't want to be alone.

My father was fun, you know. He and I would do all sorts of things together, but my favorite was when he would pop corn in his cast iron skillet over the stove, sprinkle it with just a touch of sea salt, and the two of us would sit and watch his favorite Western television shows while we enjoyed our snack.

My mother wasn't *as* fun as my father was, but when time allowed, she and I would shop the racks, have brunch together on a Saturday morning or visit Ms. Kim at the nail salon around the corner from our house for a pair of double coats. It was all fun but not nearly as fun as the time I spent with other children. So, I told myself that when I grew up and married, I would have a huge family, design all of the children's wardrobes, and even if there was only one in the bunch, I had to have a girl!

"Honey, you are carrying way too low for that to be a boy!"

my mother said when I asked her what her best guess was.

And I wanted that to be true so badly that I took her hypothesis as fact and drove Greg crazy as I shopped until I just about dropped! So, when my doctor finally confirmed what I already believed to be true, it felt great knowing that my justification to Greg about why I was ordering more than one of everything had been validated.

"Girls need options, baby," I would tell him when yet another package of clothes or shoes arrived at the house.

There was nothing that I wouldn't have done to be her mother. There was nothing that I wouldn't have given. And it broke my heart into a billion pieces to know that all of my belly caresses and sweet, tender talks to her at random hours throughout the day… all of the prayers for her well-being… all of the shopping, the arranging, the dreams I had for her future and for ours… the search for the perfect pediatrician… the arguments over powder pink or mellow yellow… were all in… in vain! They were all in vain.

We agreed to call her Holly, after my great-grandmother on my father's side, rest her soul. And Elaine for a middle name, like Ms. Evelyn's. I would have kept her hair in its' natural state like my mother always kept mine, and I would have always encouraged her to do the same as I handed the responsibility over to her as she aged. We would have home-schooled her because Greg and I had agreed that it was the only way to guarantee the level of education that we desired for her. We hadn't had enough time to work out the details between our careers, but if things weren't as they were, we would have been ready. She would have been inquisitive and bold, like me. And if I won the bet, she would have had double dimples, just like her daddy.

Instead, my sweet baby girl laid lifeless in my arms as the pain in my eyes trickled down onto her cold and colorless body. My poor, *poor* girl. My Holly. My dream. I never did find out the real cause of my premature labor or why, even after having a strong heartbeat in utero just moments before my Caesarean, she was stillborn. For a long time, I blamed myself. *I* was responsible for her survival and I had failed at doing the only thing that really mattered.

There was a silent but mutual understanding between Greg and I when we returned home from the hospital after spending four days and nights in the maternity ward. I mean, can you imagine —after being made to mourn your own child— being surrounded by an abundance of healthy, thriving newborns and their glowing mothers? *That* was hell on Earth!

The child we had expected to welcome into our lives had come and gone in the blink of an eye and all that remained was the evidence of her conception. A box full of positive pregnancy tests because I just couldn't believe the news. A closet full of maternity pieces because my belly had outgrown my regular wardrobe. And an office full of parenting pamphlets and manuals I'd planned on using if times ever got tough. It was horrible, and all I really wanted to do was curl up in my bed and cry until the memory of her faded. But my fear was just that - that it *would* fade, and the truth is that, even now, I feel tremendous guilt because sometimes, in the loops of life, I forget that she ever even existed.

This is the moment that *I* changed; at least, that's what I tell myself to somehow justify the shift in my circumstances. It changed Greg, too, in ways that I could never fully understand because, naturally, our roles just weren't the same. He loved her in his own fatherly way. And I know the memories of that time still haunt him, but he has done a better job carrying on than I have, or so it seems. Life's changes are inevitable, that's for sure. But all changes come with challenges now, don't they?

6

The Challenge

Whenever she would find me lost between the pages, she would make her way over and practically beg me to stop what I was doing and play with her. I removed my reading glasses, relaxed into my seat and smiled as her tiny fingertips fidgeted against my shoulders. I *hated* pulling away from my writing once I found my rhythm, but I knew that the days of her wanting me to play her childish games were numbered. At least that's what my mother, Greg's mother, and all of the other important women in my life told me.

"Close your eyes, Mommy!" she demanded as she began to spin my chair around in circles.

Unable to tell her no, I obliged.

"Okay, baby," I said, "mommy's here. I am all yours."

She was my weakness. She was my everything. And as her sweet Southern-kissed voice delivered a resounding rendition of "Ring Around the Rosie" and the cool and unexpected breeze in the room brushed gently over my face, I was reminded of the innocence of a much younger, carefree and candid version of myself. My imperfectly platted pigtails - because I, like my mother, was never much of a braider. My soft, buttery brown skin - before puberty came, wreaked havoc on my face and left me to pick up the pieces. And the sweet smell of curiosity inside an exciting world you've only just begun to explore. She was my spitting image, yet, an image even more beautiful than my mind's eye could have conceived.

But I couldn't take all of the credit. Aside from Greg's dimples, she had his heart. One that never knew a stranger and remained open even when closing was the wiser option. One that dreamed of saving the world from itself and from the strangers who threatened to destroy it. Eyes that only saw the best in everyone, even when mine suspected otherwise. And a soul that shed tears for the homeless because she, although young, understood that life wasn't always fair to those who deserved it most. We had done good, Greg and I. And I was, with no doubt, proud to be her mother.

"Now," she whispered ever so softly as she slowed down the chair. "Open your eyes, Mommy. Open your eyes and look around!" she insisted.

And when I did, my heart broke all over again as I realized that I was alone and had been dreaming all along. It had not been the first time, nor would it be the last. And sometimes, I wondered if I was actually dreaming or just hoping that when I opened my eyes, Holly's nonexistence *was* the dream. Back then, I never wanted to open my eyes because I knew that if I did, there was a chance that I really *was* just dreaming of her. But I could never keep them shut because I couldn't live with myself knowing that I kept her waiting for me. You see, the tangling of my web started years ago. And some days, I was sure of that, while other days, I was sure of nothing.

The reality was that it had been seven months, sixteen days, twenty-nine hours and exactly two minutes since I had written a single word in my latest novel. Between mourning the loss of Holly and struggling to keep up with the life I had already built for myself, I guess *I* was the last person my characters wanted to take advice from. Because despite my painless presentation, I was hurting in ways that felt foreign to me. Foreign! Because up until that point, everyone that I had ever truly loved had been within my reach. Even my grandmother, Ivory —who had been deceased for many years— left a piece of herself with me. So, even in *her* absence, her stories, her voice and her lessons remained. Please understand that, for the very first time in my entire life, I had completely lost control! And my subconscious was stuck living a life that I would never have, no matter how badly I wanted it. Damnit, I hate talking about this shit! I'm sorry. I'm *really* sorry.

Some days, I would go sit in my office and reminisce about her last few kicks. The feeling of knowing that all was well before it wasn't, you know. The sunshine before the storm, if you will. On other days, I would just sit there with my computer powered on. Lifting then lowering my fingers over the keyboard as thoughts and ideas exited my muddled mind just as quickly as they'd entered. But I held on to hope, I suppose. What other options did I have?

Greg and I spent two whole weeks inside together after everything happened. It was nice. The bonding, you know. We stayed up late and watched movies made before anyone cared which cameras were used. We ate chocolate edibles every night and binged on peanut butter cups, banana bread and spicy barbecue-flavored kettle chips. And in the mornings, we would shower together, count down the days before my surgical bandages were removed, then munch on fried fish, lemonade and whatever the hell else we had ordered for delivery the nights prior. But that time had come to an end. Greg was back to business, and I was back to… something.

I had grown accustomed to being alone in the house during the day while Greg worked. I used to spend my days writing new stories, taking business calls and planning my next set of moves. And as long as my net worth was less than one billion dollars, there were always moves to be made! But lately, I had become very anxious. I was bored. And I felt lonely. And the one thing that had always been my refuge had me questioning if I was a *real writer*, anyway. Imposter Syndrome? Sure. Lost? Definitely.

For months, I had carried company around inside of my body, so even when I was alone, it never *felt* that way. What I found interesting, however, was that even though I knew loneliness very well as an only child, not having Holly anymore made me feel more lonely than I had ever felt. I think I believed that she was the answer to my prayers growing up. *She* would be the beginning of this grand family that I dreamed of having. And now, that was all over and I just didn't know what to do with it.

But then, my manager called. Aside from the occasional email check-in to make sure that she hadn't unknowingly been fired, I had not heard Tanya's chipper voice in months. I also hadn't delivered any new drafts in months, so honestly, I had stopped expecting to hear from her altogether.

"Hey, Tanya!" I exclaimed.

"It's so good to hear from you," I said, pretending to be in good spirits.

"Lauren, hi!" she eagerly replied. "You sound great!"

I did it! I had fooled her.

"I've got some exciting news to share with you!" she said.

And she did.

She told me that my last book series had landed in the hands of the most respected book publisher in the industry, Reverent! I could not believe my ears! For many years, I had maintained widespread success as a self-published author with no real desire to go mainstream. My money flowed in abundance, I told the stories I wanted to tell and I answered to no one. And I preferred it that way. But sometime in the previous year, Tanya suggested we try a different approach with the new series. Rather than jumping in and doing it all myself, like I always did, she asked me to trust her to get a new set of eyes on my work, just to see what would happen. Tanya had always believed in me, so I trusted her direction and did as she suggested. But never in a trillion years would I have expected Reverent to be that set of eyes.

Over the next year, my career took off, going places I never dreamed it would. Some I never even knew existed. My first stop was Wake Up!, the hottest morning news talk show in the nation at the time. The producers of the show wanted to interview the most influential writer in the industry and with Reverent pushing my book series to bestseller status at all the top bookstores and on nearly every national *and* international list in just a matter of weeks, Wake Up!, and at least one hundred other news sources around the globe wanted to sit down and talk with *me*! Can you believe that?

I had gone from independent interest to global mogul in no time, which left very little time to drown in my depression. For a while, I reveled in the rush because it required no real effort from me. Effort that I, quite frankly, didn't believe I had left to give. *They* controlled my schedule. Greg handled our personal affairs. And all I needed to do, both professionally and personally, was show up, smile and answer questions about stories that were birthed long before the tragedy. I traveled constantly - Ghana, Peru, Nova Scotia, Italy and Germany, among others, and my goal of visiting every state in the country had been reached in just a few short months.

I couldn't go into a single supermarket or department store without being recognized. Greg wasn't a big fan of the fame, but he did enjoy not having to make reservations or wait in line when we would go out to dinner. I didn't care much about the fame either, but I did understand that it came with the territory, so I embraced it. My dream had always been to reach and inspire people everywhere with my writing and Reverent had opened that world for me. And there I was, on top, and I refused to fall.

I have to admit, though, I was nervous as hell as I waited to be escorted onstage for my interview with Wake Up!. My palms were clammy, I may or may not have had to pee and my fear was that the *real* me wouldn't live up to my audience's expectations. Sure, I had been interviewed before. I was no stranger to answering questions about my work. But never had I been interviewed in front of a live studio audience with nearly the entire world waiting to hear from me, some cheering me on, others chanting for my professional demise. At least, that's what I imagined.

"You're gonna do great. They already love you, baby," Greg assured me as he held my shaky hands.

Greg never really left my side, you know? Even when I left my own.

"Lauren, we're ready for you," one of the production assistants said as she waited to take me on.

I closed my eyes, took a deep breath, smiled, pulled myself together and followed her. I'll never forget the moment I walked out and faced that crowd. Their eyes lit up as I strutted onto the stage. They howled like I was this big-time celebrity or... or like they *knew* me. On a personal level, you know? They shouted as I waved both hands at them. They were honored to share space with me. And my heart was filled with gratitude. I was seen, I had been heard and not a single person in that room expected me to be anything more than a storyteller. It was nice. And it was only the beginning.

* * *

"Hell yes! That's what I'm talking about!" Greg exclaimed as we climbed into bed that night.

"Baby, can you believe this is happening?" I asked him.

But just as he opened his mouth to respond, my adrenaline cut him off.

"I mean, all those late nights—" I said.

"Early mornings—" he interrupted.

"Tears—" I recalled.

"Fears that I told you were completely unnecessary because you are a beast!" he declared with a grin as gigantic as the geosphere.

"I am, right?" I playfully questioned.

"Fuck yeah, you are!" he confirmed.

"Fuck yes, I am," I said as we both shared a laugh.

My adrenaline settled down as Greg's warm hands began to massage my stiff neck.

"You are the sexiest novelist I have ever met in my life," he claimed.

There was never a dry moment with Greg and as long as he was around, laughter was inevitable.

"Boy, you don't even know any other novelists!" I replied.

"Yes, I do," he said.

"Name one…" I challenged.

"Mrs. Mistovich!" he fired back.

"What?! Who in the hell is that?!" I asked.

"She was my English professor in undergrad," he explained. "She was a novelist and she was not sexy at all. She was actually very ugly."

"You are just stupid! And wrong! So wrong!" I told him.

He went on to tell me how proud he was of me and of all that I had accomplished. That… that he always knew that I had something so special and that he was so happy that I had finally gotten the chance to show the *world* what he had known all along. Greg was my number one supporter and I was his, although, in the heat of my exhilaration, I had almost forgotten to do *my* part.

"Veenhuis! I'm *so* stupid," I exclaimed after realizing that I had just gone on and on about myself. "I almost forgot about your biggest potential client ever!" I said.

His silence spoke volumes, or so I thought.

"Oh no, babe!" I sympathized.

"I tried," he humbly replied.

"So, what happened?" I softly inquired, careful not to agitate him. "Did they decide to go with another firm?"

But suddenly, under that sly, knee-weakening grin that first captivated me all those years ago, lied a prank.

"I know good and well you did not just lie to me!" I said as he chuckled.

"I got you good, didn't I?" he said.

I couldn't believe that shit! There I was, trying to console his sad ass, and he was lying the whole time. He had become the exclusive Wealth Management Consultant for the *entire* Veenhuis portfolio! *My* husband! I had watched him build that company from the ground up, with just a dream and a drive that only one other man in my life could ever compete with, my father. Indeed, that asshole had gotten me good!

But I love him, still. Even though things… you know? And that night, we made love for the first time in a long time out of pure passion, *love* and admiration for the people we had grown into. We weren't grieving. We weren't broken. We weren't burdened by our losses. We were ready for the road ahead… and in the heat of the moment, we were *foolish*.

Several weeks passed, and my long list of appearances and speaking engagements was well underway. I was living "the life," and no one could stop me! But no matter how many eight-hour nights I slept, I found it incredibly difficult to keep my eyes open at the most random of times. Gina was the first to notice when I dozed off during our discussion over dinner.

"Girl, you need to take a test," she said.

"A *test?*" I groggily replied.

"Yeah, a damn pregnancy test!" she clarified. "Bitch, your ass just fell asleep mid-sentence and the server didn't even bring your food yet! And wipe that drool off your face. That shit is embarrassing!" she lectured.

Gina never did give a damn about saying whatever came to mind. That's why I love her so much. And to be completely honest, I had been so distracted with my schedule that it hadn't even registered to me that I had not updated my period tracker in almost two months! Gina was right. Something was off, and there was but one way to find out the truth. I just didn't think that would happen as quickly as it did.

You probably won't believe this, and honestly, I shouldn't have even been shocked because Gina has always been crazy, but this girl lied and said that she was going to the bathroom, took off on foot to the drugstore at the corner, and came back with a purse full of pregnancy tests! She claimed they were "buy one, get one free," but I didn't believe that.

"Here you go," she said as she handed me one after another. "I'll wait," she said as she smirked and blotted the sweat from her forehead.

And she did.

As I sat in that bathroom awaiting my fate, my feet tapping rhythmically against the hardwood floor, my anxiety was met with a myriad of unexpected emotions. After what had happened with Holly, did I even *want* to have another baby? Was my body able to handle another pregnancy? What if I *was* pregnant? Would I lose that baby, too? What about my career? Was Greg ready for this? Did either of us have the time to be parents? I wasn't in love with the idea of having an abortion, but in that moment, I wasn't opposed to it. Had I grieved Holly long enough? Had I selfishly let her go? My mental madness made three minutes feel like an hour. And then… it happened.

"I knew it, I knew it, I knew it!" Gina proclaimed as she grinned from ear to ear.

"You always had nice skin… except for that one year, but *girl…*" she carried on.

As Gina reveled in my revelation, I struggled to accept the actuality of it all. I didn't *feel* happy. In fact, I felt… conflicted. And that was the challenge. *How* was I supposed to do this? I had convinced myself that I had moved forward and that life was better than ever, but the fact of the matter was that, in that moment, as blood rushed through my veins, I was reminded that I was *human*. And my story was headed toward a climax that I wasn't at all prepared for. And I needed water… lots of water. And more bread and butter. Oh, boy. It was a challenge, indeed.

7

The Climax

When Lauren told me that she was pregnant, I didn't know how I was supposed to feel, to be honest with you. Before everything happened with Holly, I always *knew* that we would have a big family. Lots of kids running around, a big old yard, table full of people eating pancakes and sausages together on the weekends. The whole nine yards, right? Lauren wanted it, too. We had talked about it since we were teenagers, and for a long time, we planned for it. That's how we ended up buying that house in the first place.

Once Lauren agreed to marry me, we started looking at different places in different areas, but it wasn't as simple as just finding a house we liked and putting in an offer. It needed to have enough bedrooms to fit the family we planned on raising. It needed to have enough bathrooms so that nobody ever had to fight over toilets or showers. It needed to be in a nice neighborhood with highly-ranked schools and access to various extracurricular activities so that our kids could be well-rounded.

Both Lauren and I really wanted to live in a Black neighborhood or at least one that was diverse, but those neighborhoods didn't really provide what we needed. So, we settled on WillowBrooke Row - a quiet, affluent, family-friendly subdivision with enough room for the family we were planning to have. The only downside was that the schools were white as hell, and they still didn't offer the quality of education that we wanted for our children, so we decided that when the time came, we would homeschool.

I don't think most people even think about losing their first child or any child, for that matter, so when that shit happens to you, it's like, wow… that shit *really* happened. It complicates things. A person can go from being happy and full of joy, excited for the future and everything, to being completely torn apart and scared, for real. That's how I felt. All mixed up. Nervous as hell. Always worried about Lauren and the baby, hoping she wasn't pushing herself too hard, you know, with her work. I didn't want her to have to put up with that shit all over again, you know? I really just wanted her to rest and let me take care of her, but you know how she is. Or… *was,* anyway.

Besides, writing was her whole world and her mind was something else. That's what I love about her the most. I always will, no matter what. The way she used to tell them stories; It *consumed* her. It was like *all* of her characters lived inside of her and they were just waiting on her to give them permission to speak. And when she did… aw man, it was beautiful. It was inspiring and I felt like it was an honor to even know somebody like that, let alone share my life with her.

So yeah, things had changed quite a bit in our lives since the first pregnancy. Lauren was pretty popular before, but by that time, she couldn't leave the house without people crowding around her at some point. People were always in her business, in *our* business. And when folks started finding out that she was pregnant, it got a little crazy for a minute. My brother, Nate, used to work for this security company - Lowell's or Lool's, or something like that. He wasn't doing that type of work anymore, but he had hooked me up with his buddy, Malcolm, this guy he used to work with. He was a cool guy. Funny. Dude was short as hell, but he was built like a bull.

Nate was like, "Bro, he might be little, but people don't fuck with Malcolm like that, man." They already know what time it is!"

My brother is pretty goofy, but when it comes to judging people and their character, I trust him. Lauren thought it was stupid and pointless, but I hired Malcolm just to make sure that she was safe and protected. I couldn't always be around, but I wasn't about to let nothing happen to her, you know what I mean? That's my baby. So, when I couldn't be there, and even sometimes when I could, I brought Malcolm in to keep a lookout. And he did a great job at it.

But anyway, this time around, just to keep everything private and not have a bunch of reporters talking about shit she wasn't trying to talk about, we decided to go with a midwife instead of a doctor. That way, Lauren didn't have to worry about nobody following her up to the doctor's office or anything crazy like that. I mean, I was all for it. And when her doctor told her that she was eligible for a VBAC, well, it was settled. We were getting a midwife. She was cool, though. Her name was Alice... Robinson, I think. Black lady, middle-aged. About ye' high.

"As long as everything goes smoothly, you and I will both be right by Lauren's side when it comes time for her to have the baby, right here in the comfort of our own home," she told me.

I think the lady was friends with her mom or her aunt Edna or somebody. She had that kind of warm spirit, like somebody's mama. She was always smiling and that made both Lauren and I feel comfortable - at least for the time being. She even called and checked on Lauren to make sure she was taking her vitamins and doing her stretches at night and everything. I liked her. So yeah, that worked out alright.

Alice told us that Lauren's morning sickness would probably only last a few months, but she was nauseous for a lot longer than that. In the early mornings, mostly. Every time her stomach would get used to holding certain foods down, it would reset on her, you know, and she would be throwing up all over again. It was wild and rough on her, but I think she did pretty good with the whole pregnancy, all things considered.

Lauren had been running around, traveling like crazy, every week. Tired or not, she was committed to her career, that's for sure. She was nervous about the baby, but I think she thought that if she kept herself busy, she wouldn't be so bothered by it. So, that's what she did. I mean, she didn't slow down until she *had* to. She only had about a month or so left before her due date, and she was stubborn, so there wasn't really nothing I could do about that. Lauren was gonna do what she wanted to do, and she's always been that way. So, I just supported her the best way I could. That's how it's always been.

It was Lauren's birthday, so I wanted to do something special for her. Tanya made sure that her schedule was clear, so I had her to myself for two whole days. She was snoozing soundly in the sheets that morning when I walked in carrying a tray of fried eggs, turkey bacon and a candlelit blueberry muffin. Oh, and some orange juice, too. That was her new favorite breakfast, but I still kept my fingers crossed because we never knew what was gonna happen.

Now, I'm not the best singer in the world, but Lauren used to always tell me that I had a pretty good voice, so I cleared my throat and started singing "Happy Birthday" to her. After a while, she smiled, opened her eyes and looked up at me. Even first thing in the morning, she was so beautiful. Her hair, her skin… everything. No effort at all. Anyway, when I finished singing the song, she started clapping. I think she knew that shit didn't sound too good, but she was happy about it, and at the end of the day, that was all that mattered to me.

"Aww, thank you, babe!" she said as she waved me in for a kiss.

"Make a wish, baby," I said to her as I carefully placed the tray over the top of her belly.

She closed her eyes and started making her wish, but after about thirty seconds, she started snoring. She couldn't stay awake for nothing, at least not when it was time to. It didn't bother me, though. I understood what was happening, and if the early days of motherhood were anything like my mama told me they'd be, I knew she needed as much rest as she could get before the baby got here.

I had spent the last few weeks making plans for her birthday. It was the last one before the baby took over our lives, so I wanted to make sure that she enjoyed herself. Later that morning, Ms. Robin, her mother, came over to spend a little girl time with her. So, I used that time to finalize everything and get it all set up for the evening. I wanted it to be perfect for her.

* * *

A hot pink bandana secured her hair as she stroked the walls in a funky green color. I thought it was a rather hideous hue, but I simply turned my nose and returned my attention to organizing the closet. Lauren *did* have great taste and I hoped that this color was all a part of a bigger picture - one that I clearly could not see yet.

"Mom?" she asked.

"What?" I replied, fully aware that she was on to me.

"You don't like it, do you?" she continued.

"No, honey," I fibbed, "I like it."

But if anyone truly knew their mother, it was Lauren.

"Then why are you looking like it stinks in here?" she asked. "*I'm* not even looking like it stinks in here and it stinks everywhere!"

"Honey, it's fine, really," I chuckled, "if you like that sort of color."

"Mom?!" she exclaimed, rather annoyed with my responses.

Despite my professional background in fashion, when it came to children and the choosing of their colors, I was more traditional in my approach. I was more of a baby blue girl myself. Or orange - if one elected to venture outside of the box. I've seen striking shades of orange that looked gorgeous against brown skin. That may have been nice.

"Well, I like green," Lauren declared. "And besides, what if the sonographer is wrong and little Gregory is actually little Gretchen?"

My word! I nearly choked on my tongue!

"You name my grandchild Gretchen and I'm painting *you* green!" I warned her.

What a disgusting name! Don't you agree? Lauren found my reaction quite funny. I didn't.

I was *very* grateful for another chance to be a grandmother, although I outright refused to be identified as such. "Nana" was more fitting for a woman of my age and composition, so that's what we decided on, long before little Gregory was ever even a thought, of course. The stillbirth was difficult for all of us. It truly was. I really could not imagine going through that myself - seeing the child and knowing that it wasn't coming home with me. I rarely speak on this, but before Lauren was conceived, Kenneth and I miscarried. Twice, to be precise. Yes. It was painful, of course, but I imagine that to be somewhat of an understatement in comparison to what Lauren and Gregory had experienced. *That* was heavy, and it required a great deal of strength on Lauren's behalf to carry it.

"I can't do this, mom," she would often cry out to me when the depths of her depression pulled at her.

"It's too much," she would tell me.

I kept my phone line and my arms open to her, but I knew that with patience and a bit of grace, she really could handle it. Pardon me, but all of this reminiscing brings my mother, Ivory —rest her soul— to the forefront... how she cared for me as I struggled to overcome my maternal mishaps. She'd hold me close and stroke my tired curls like I was her little girl all over again.

"Even lavender lilies wither sometimes, Robby," she'd remind me as she sipped sweet tea from her favorite Mason jar. "But if you're patient and careful with them, they'll come back around."

My mother loved her lavender lilies just as much as she loved a good analogy. Although she never did write much, she had an incredible way with words, just like Lauren.

I can hear her now, just as clear as day. "Nothing smells

nearly as lovely as lavender. And no flower feels as loved as the lily," she'd say. "The perfect pair. Almost."

It took years to understand what she meant by that. We were close, my mother and I. I could tell her all of my secrets, we both adored patterned scarves of a particular feel and even when I doubted myself, she always ensured that I came out on the other side. But there was an unspoken distance between us that only time and experience could find a way to explain.

I think that many of us take having our mothers in our lives for granted. I certainly did. But my mother didn't have that privilege because her mother's demons drove her down dark roads that all ended at the same destination. And sadly, my mother's relationships with the other women in her life did little to fill the void of her mother's absence. So, in a significant sense, she was a motherless child. And while I cannot relate to that, my own experiences as a mother —the innate bond that Lauren and I share and all that comes along with that— have revealed to me the painful impossibility of being one's complete self without a connection to the very person that brought you here.

In other words, that unspoken distance between my mother and I was nothing more than the distance she felt from hers and her natural inability to process it. And just knowing that she died with so much untreated trauma in her heart breaks mine. I know this isn't about me or about my mother, but I do appreciate you for listening. Those memories always have a way of showing up without warning.

You know, I think that Lauren's publishing deal arrived in perfect timing for her and I think she would agree with me. Sure, she was quite vulnerable then, but I felt like she needed something bigger than herself to propel her forward out of her slump. Does that make sense? I sure hope it didn't come across the wrong way. I do find myself convicted of that on occasion.

But Kenneth and I felt overwhelmingly proud of Lauren and all that she had achieved in life. We always knew that she was capable of greatness, but she had transcended into *magnificence,* and neither of us could have been more satisfied. All of us were, really.

I'm so sorry, dear… I forget how we landed on the topic of her accomplishments. Oh, that's right… the new baby, yes. I couldn't wait to hold him. To look into his sweet little eyes. You know, Kenneth and I stocked a closet full of clothing for him in our home, in an assortment of sizes to accommodate him as he thrived. It was fun for both of us and we were thrilled!

I could tell by Lauren's antsiness, however, that she was worried about how the pregnancy would progress. So, I think she clung to the thing that she had the most control over, which was her career. She did all of the things to prepare for the baby's arrival, but it never really seemed like she was all that connected to the idea of being a mother again. Sure, the thought of having a new baby after one has lost one might be rather rousing to some mothers. But for Lauren… I think she felt unsure of herself and of the baby more than anything else. And I think it backfired, I really do. It was almost as if she hadn't properly bonded with him, or perhaps she couldn't bring herself to do it. Nevertheless, the child was coming due, and despite her feelings, she, like most mothers, did what needed to be done.

* * *

Greg had outdone himself! I'm still not really sure how he was able to pull it off, but he secured my all-time favorite singer to perform her greatest hits right alongside her talented team of musicians! Candle lights flickered every which way I turned… polished packages with pretty bows placed picturesquely around me. And because sometimes I held food down but most times I didn't, he hired a dynamic team of sous chefs to prepare whatever dishes I desired that evening, and he kept a pocketful of ginger chews handy, in case my nausea got the best of me. It was very thoughtful of him.

We hadn't spent much time alone in the backyard since our wedding reception, so that night was even more special. The mood was perfect, and if I weren't already pregnant, there was a good chance that I would have conceived afterward. I was a lucky woman, and as terrified as I was about becoming a mother, I did the best I could to stay present that night.

"I am so happy that I get to love you for the rest of my life," I told Greg as he held me closely in his arms.

The moonlight and the stars smiled down on us as we cuddled on the most comfortable cushions I had ever sat on. I meant to ask him where he found them, but I never did get around to it. He smiled and kissed the top of my head as he gently guided it onto his chest. It was the best feeling in the world.

It took me a long time to fall asleep that night, which was unusual for me, especially then. My belly had grown so large that I found it challenging to settle into a comfortable position. Usually, a climax helped me to relax and drift off with little effort but not that night. While Greg rested peacefully next to me, I tossed and turned for hours before ultimately settling down. But I didn't sleep for very long. A familiar gripe in my groin startled me out of my slumber! My eyes popped open and as I arose in anguish, my commanding cry tossed Greg out of his trance! I reached back, grabbed his shirt and yanked him forward with more strength than I had ever exerted!

"What's wrong, baby?!" he asked.

"He's coming!!!" I exclaimed as I crippled over, sweat beads dripping from my face.

And no doubt, this time, he was.

Greg and I had planned for a water birth. I had done a ton of research on the topic and our midwife, Alice, was in full support of our decision. I had also found a very nice, leak-proof birthing pool that was fully equipped with all of the bells and whistles, those I might need and those I definitely wouldn't, but I liked the style, so I bought it anyway. There was but one tiny little problem: It was May twenty-seventh, an entire week before the day the pool was scheduled to be delivered.

As I laid in bed battling what felt like a beast in my belly, impatiently awaiting the arrival of Alice from wherever the hell she was coming from, I found myself riddled with worry of the unknown in between contractions. There was little difference between the pain I felt that night and the pain I remembered from before. So, in the back of my mind, I couldn't help but wonder if this too would all be in vain. One moment the pain was so incredibly intense that I couldn't stand to think beyond that very moment. But less than one minute later, my head went haywire, proposing worst-case scenarios and unthinkables that I couldn't help but think about. It was the most dreadful experience of my life and I was more miserable than I cared to be.

I watched as Greg followed Alice's lead over the phone, gathering washcloths and bath towels, rubbing alcohol and an assortment of items for me and the baby. He was pretty tense; I could tell by the crinkle between his brows. He had played it cool throughout my pregnancy, but it was the first time that he didn't seem very cool at all. And for some reason, that made me feel a little better, knowing that I wasn't the only unhappy one in the room. I could only imagine the thoughts that harbored inside his head. I wasn't the only one who had been left scarred by Holly's stillbirth, and I got the feeling that this type of busy work was a crutch for the emotions Greg wasn't prepared to deal with.

If it had not been for that mattress protector, our bed might have been permanently ruined because just as soon as Greg left to let Alice inside the house, my water broke. I know this sounds silly, but I remember feeling a bit embarrassed by that, like I had wet myself under different circumstances and that everyone would find out my big secret. But as Alice rushed into the room, peeled my legs apart and slid her gloved hand inside my vagina, I quickly remembered that in childbirth, there are no secrets.

"It won't be long now, Lauren," Alice confirmed as she removed her hand, discarded her glove and gently patted me on the knee.

Hearing those words provided a bit of relief because I just wasn't sure how much more I could handle. My contractions grew closer and more robust. I had become persistently nauseous, my legs ached and the pressure in my lower back felt like my child was going to break out of my skin at any given moment. I was indeed in active labor, and that was the real commencement of this entire ordeal. I think.

8

The Commencement

I had ushered more unborns into the world than my mind had space to store, yet, I will never forget Lauren Winters or the day she gave birth to her son. Lauren was my favorite of all the mothers. She was smart, successful and well put-together but ever so humble and just as sweet as pie. She was a breath of fresh air and because of my fondness of her, I worried about her, probably as much as she worried about herself. But from a different perspective, you understand? We had something in common, too, Lauren and I, so when she shared her story with me, I knew how she felt because one day, many moons ago, I felt that exact same way.

I had just celebrated my nineteenth birthday and my husband, Roy, and I found out shortly after that I was pregnant. Okay, now, listen to me: I was happy about it, but I was scared, too. There I was, young, broke and married, and in less than a year, I was going to be somebody's mother. So, as happy as I was, a part of me just wanted to take a step back and force Roy to wear protection, but hey, there we were. And we had some sorting out to do!

I was the eldest of twelve children, so I didn't have any worries about how to take care of the baby. I had been an integral part of my mother's village all of my life. If a baby was hungry and a breast wasn't available, I knew to pull milk from mama's collection in the back of the freezer. Mama usually had two children in diapers at the same time, so you know what that meant, don't you? It meant that I learned how to change two diapers at once! You see, if you put one baby on each side of you with their legs and feet facing one another, they'll start playing footsie, which, believe it or not, is fun for babies. Even more, it's an easy way for you to get in there, clean them up quickly and get a new diaper strapped on them before they even realize they're in the nude. My grandmother taught me that because *she* was the eldest of seventeen children and had every trick you could imagine stored up her sleeve.

I knew a lot about taking care of children, but I didn't know what was really required to be a mother. The work felt… different. I did pretty much all of the things that my mother did, but I hadn't *felt* all of the emotions she felt because until I had gotten myself pregnant, I had only been a caretaker. So, I stressed about it, probably more than I should have. And as tired as I was in the early months of my pregnancy, I didn't sleep. I couldn't. I didn't do what I should have done to take care of myself; that's what I'm getting at. I didn't *feel* like I was ready to be anybody's mother, but when that Emergency Room doctor told me that my baby had been stillborn, well, I surely wasn't prepared for that either. This isn't really about me, so I'll leave that for another time. All I'm saying to you is that when Lauren told me about her baby girl, I knew that pain, and I knew it well. And after going on to have four more children, myself, I knew exactly what she was going through with her pregnancy.

The memory of Lauren's labor still feels close, as if it were yesterday. As she laid on her side, heavily perspiring from the pressure within, Gregory held her hand, soothing her as I massaged her lower back. She was a *very* brave woman, as she labored without medical intervention. That was her decision, of course, and I intended to support her. But, I have to admit, it was a rare choice. I've cared for a lot of pregnant women, and even those who initially chose to deliver naturally usually wound up changing their minds once that labor turns on. But not Lauren. Nope. She stuck to her guns, even when I would've pulled the trigger, myself.

Lauren's scream shook the room! Hell, it shook the house, and that was a big old pretty house. Immaculate! Sharp! And it was as if all of Lauren's pains - physical, emotional, mental and spiritual were all vying for attention at the exact same time. And once that labor turned on, Lauren rode those waves like a sailor! And poor Gregory, he stood right by her side, helpless, concerned and understandably emotional. But he did alright, bless his heart.

You know, a lot of people don't think that men have the same kinds of feelings as women do when it comes to these types of things, but I know they do. Really, I think it's society telling these men that they can't cry when they're hurting because it'll make them look like punks or something, but that's not true. My father was good about teaching my brothers to express themselves, whether they were feeling happy, sad, somewhere in between, or someplace farther than any of *us* had ever traveled to. He validated all of it!

"When you hide your feelings, you hide yourself," he would always say.

And he was right. What sense does it make to live in a world where you can't be the person you really are? Where you can't feel what you really feel? We're all human and we all feel *something* at one time or another. Now think about this: If at the center of *each one of us* is emotion, what is the point of pretending that none of that exists? You don't have to answer me, just think about it. All I'm saying to you is that the emotion in me could feel Gregory's emotions, and I just wanted him to know that it was alright, whatever he was feeling.

"Trust me, Gregory," I assured him.

"I'm trying," he said, "but I know my wife and something's not right. Please, can you just take another look?" he begged.

How could I object to that? No one with a heart could, and I had a little bit of concern myself.

"Lauren," I prepared her, "I'm going to help you turn onto your back so I can check your progress again, alright?"

"I'm right here, baby," Gregory whispered to her. "Just breathe. That's it. You're doing so good," he said.

Gregory was so supportive and loving and kind to her. And although she *was* doing good, my examination revealed that the umbilical cord was wrapped tightly around the baby's neck. Each contraction created more strain, which made it even tighter. I explained to both Lauren and Gregory that I would need to deliver their baby's head first then I would be able to assess the situation from there.

I apologized because Lord knows, I hated to do it, but I needed Gregory to step out of the room. I felt awful about that, but I required Lauren's utmost cooperation and trust, and my experience showed me that partners were often a distraction in dire instances. And given the circumstances, this was indeed dire.

"I'm not leaving her alone!" he asserted.

"Gregory, please. It's for the best," I assured him.

I knew that he understood, but with his experience, it was hard for him to accept it. As he stepped back, his emotions nearly broke him down completely. He struggled to control his breath. God only knows what possibilities haunted him. Poor, poor Gregory. I felt sorry for him; I did. But as difficult as it was for him to accept what was happening, he listened and he left, like I'd asked him to. I believe he trusted me, as much as he could, that is. And as I did everything in my power to ensure a safe and successful delivery of their child, I couldn't help but wonder how Gregory was managing on the other side of that door.

* * *

I couldn't stop pacing the floor as I battled with the bullshit that bounced around inside of my brain. As much as I wanted everything to be alright in that room, there was just no way to be sure. And being on the other side of that door sure as hell didn't help the situation. I don't even think *worry* was the right word. I was... *everything*. I was as terrified of losing another baby just as much as I was afraid of losing Lauren.

I thought, "What if the baby made it, but Lauren didn't?"

That *was* a possibility, you know? What... what the fuck was I gonna do without her? I couldn't *imagine* having to live without Lauren in my life. And what if it was the other way around again and Lauren and I were left to deal with another loss that I didn't think either one of us could handle? Lauren was my everything and we had our whole lives to look forward to. But there was something about being on the other side of that door… something about not knowing how things were gonna work themselves out, not being able to lend a hand or to at least see if a hand was even needed. There was something about that, and I hated that feeling so much.

Yeah, I was excited about the chance to hold my son, my namesake. But at the same damn time, I was anxious because I felt like there was a strong possibility that he would never even take his first breath. It was real fucked up. I thought about calling my mama or Lauren's parents, but to be honest, I didn't even want to pull them into it yet, not knowing how it would turn out. It was rough on me, man. I can't even lie. Damn, it was rough. All the screaming and crying… it just ate away at my heart. So, I just closed my eyes and let the tears roll while I waited.

* * *

I don't think that mothers get enough credit, to be quite frank. We actually bring new humans into the world, and that is no small task. If it were not for mothers, none of us would even be here. There would *be* no human population, and when you put it that way, I think that to simply overlook the power that mothers possess is pure ignorance. Whether or not one chooses an epidural to aid in the process is a personal choice, yes. But the amount of strength and courage that it requires to carry and *deliver* a child… no one talks about that. Not enough, at least. And witnessing that power, in full force… well, that is why I've been a midwife all of these years. And the strength that Lauren showed that night was nothing short of incredible.

Lauren's delivery took quite a while longer than I expected it to, but after a good bit of focus and effort, I pulled the head of a flimsy, lifeless baby out of her womb. A beautifully brown little boy with a head full of the deepest, jet-black waves I've ever seen on a baby. With the cord wrapped tightly around his neck, I carefully cut it free and prepared to proceed with the delivery.

"Ok, honey. You're almost there," I reassured her. "On the very next contraction, I need you to give it *everything* you've got. Alright?"

And indeed, she did, pushing through that pain like a warrior as we delivered the remainder of her son's body from her uterus. The room sat silent for a moment as the small child laid still, almost as if he was asleep, unaware that he had been relocated.

"What's wrong with him, Alice?" Lauren inquired as I placed him on the bed next to her while I suctioned mucus from his mouth. "Why isn't he crying?!" she demanded to know.

But the application of a gentle pressure onto his small chest and a mature breath of fresh air into his young lungs quickly settled her worries as his strong cry soon commanded the room! Young Gregory William Winters, Jr. was alive, he was well, and he was, at last, cozy in his mother's arms. An entire five pounds, fifteen ounces worth of alive and well, to be exact. And I could not have been more proud of Lauren and all that she had accomplished in that bedroom. Even though *I* had not delivered my second child as naturally as she had done, I wholeheartedly understood the feeling that came with making it to the finish line. And Lauren had done it with flying colors.

"Thank you, Alice," she uttered as she held on tightly to her baby boy.

The pleasure was all mine.

But I couldn't forget about dear Gregory. Tears fell from his face as I opened that door and welcomed him back into the bedroom. Relieved and highly rewarded, he approached Lauren, gently wiped her tears with his hand and kissed her on the lips.

"I'm so proud of you, baby," he told her just before lifting the small child from her arms and into his.

"Hey, son," he greeted the newborn. "I'm so glad you made it, man. Daddy's gonna take good care of you, alright?" he assured him.

It was the sweetest thing and Lauren and I smiled, both inside and out, at the sight of pure love. And all was exactly as it should have been. At least for the time being.

* * *

I took some time off work to bond with the baby and to help Lauren recover from the delivery. I was real happy, man. I had my wife next to me and I had my son in my arms and they were both breathing. I felt like a lucky man and I never wanted that feeling to leave. Lauren nursed the baby and slept all the time, so I kept the lights dim and I made sure that the volume on the TV was low anytime I was in the room with her. I just wanted her to be comfortable and to be able to rest.

Everybody was excited to come over and see Gregory, you know. Both of our families, all our friends. And I think that some paparazzi must've figured out that Alice was the midwife because we started getting all of this fan mail and random gifts from strangers. Our family and friends had to wait to visit, though because Lauren didn't really want anybody at the house yet, so people sent us flowers and balloons, you know, just showing her some love and wishing us well.

Anyway, Alice had called and said that she wanted to stop by and see how Lauren and Gregory were coming along. I hadn't really seen anybody since he was born, except the neighbors when I would pick up the mail and take the trash out, so I was just happy to see another human being.

"I see that little Gregory is clean, smelling good and is doing as he should," said Alice the first day she came for a visit. "Very well. And how are you, Gregory?" she asked.

I told her that I was good and that I was just tired because the days had been long and the nights had been shorter than I needed them to be. I told her that I was fine, though, but that I was concerned about Lauren.

"She's been sleeping a lot," I told her as she checked Lauren's vitals. "She wakes up when it's time to feed the baby and she pretty much goes right back to sleep afterwards. Is that normal?" I asked.

"Having a baby takes a lot out of a woman," she explained. "Lauren's body has been through a very traumatic experience, and some mothers just require more time to bounce back than others," she continued. "Her vitals are all normal. She looks quite healthy. And I am sure that Lauren will be back to her old self in no time."

I sure hoped so.

* * *

I pretended to be asleep when Alice came to visit us after Gregory was born. But I was far from asleep. I was very much awake, although I wished I wasn't. In fact, I found it difficult to sleep because every time I closed my eyes, it felt as if it were time to rise and shine again, and Gregory's need-to-feed schedule left very little time to actually shine.

I would often lie there wondering if I had made a poor decision and hating myself for even thinking that if, during dinner with Gina that day —when the thought of abortion meddled in my mind as I awaited the results of my pregnancy test— I should have entertained the idea a bit longer. It wasn't that I regretted my decision to continue on with my pregnancy. It was just that I felt this sadness inside of me that wasn't there before Gregory was there with me, and I wanted *that* gone. I wanted to feel what I felt when I first held him, but I no longer did. I wanted to feel the joy the mothers in my parenting books felt when they held *their* babies for the first time and every time after that. I wanted to feel like Gregory was the best thing that ever happened to me. I wanted to feel… connected to him because this feeling that weighed me down brought on a sense of disconnection. And I wanted it gone. All of it… just gone.

I don't know how I *expected* to feel in the days after giving birth; I just thought that what I was feeling didn't match what other mothers must have felt. I didn't feel normal. Sure, I had heard about the "Baby Blues." But I had never known of anyone who looked like me having them, so I knew *that* couldn't be what I was experiencing. None of the books I had read, none of the magazine articles, none of the celebrity interviews had mentioned *this* feeling, not for women like me.

A part of me felt grateful that Gregory had survived and was doing so well. But a darker part of me struggled to hold back tears for reasons unbeknownst to me. My physical strength restored itself as the days passed. My mind, however, was trapped inside of this… cyclone, and the faster it spun, the more difficult I found it to control.

9

The Cyclone

I come from a long line of strong-minded, although sometimes narrow-minded Black women who believed in hard work, independence and self-sufficiency. All the elders believed that a woman should not only work hard to have her own, they believed that accepting things from other people was a sign of weakness. And in my family, the strength of a woman is a badge of honor. To hell with weakness!

So, when it came time for Greg to be born and later on, Nate, having a baby shower was simply out of the question. As a matter of fact, I never even asked for one because I already knew what my mama was gonna say because I heard how deep she cut into my older sister when she asked about having one for her baby.

"That's *your* child, Carol Ann," she told her. "You can shower him all you want to when he get here. That ain't *our* job," she said.

And I didn't even let it simmer in my mind back then because I didn't want my mama thinking that I was trying to get nothing from nobody that I didn't already pay for with my own money.

It was a different time and I worked hard to provide for mine, even before Harvey passed because that's all I knew. But when Robin asked me if I wanted to help her plan a baby shower for Lauren, well, I was honored because the truth was that if things had been different back when I was expecting, I think I would've wanted the same for myself.

Now, unfortunately, Lauren wound up having lil' Greg before any of us thought she would. So, Robin and I talked about it and we decided to postpone the baby shower until after Lauren was back on her feet. Childbearing ain't easy and them boys, whew honey, them boys'll wear you out! Especially when you're breastfeeding. I nursed each of mine for about six months a piece and I don't think I slept a wink the whole time, child! I was running around looking like a chicken with his head cut off!

I couldn't wait to be a grandmama, though. I just felt awful when that first child didn't make it. Awful! Broke my heart, watching Greg and Lauren go through that. Lord works in mysterious ways and that was truly a mystery. It really did a number on that girl, too. Tell you the truth, I think she was depressed. But when they told me that she was pregnant again, I was thankful that they got another shot at it. Knew it wasn't gon' be easy for 'em, but once they ripped that bandage off and could see how that wound had healed, I knew they'd be alright. I hoped they would, anyhow.

The baby was born at home, in their bedroom. The way Greg tells it, the midwife was gentle and took good care of Lauren so, it seemed to me like it was a good idea. Lauren wasn't feeling up for visitors at first so, we all stayed away for a while. Sometimes Nate would come by the house and I'd fix my hair up real nice so he could take a video of me to send over to 'em - just so they'd know they was on my mind. But I sure did miss 'em and I was ready to hold that baby! Even more so when Greg sent me a picture and showed me how much he favored him. Looked just like Greg did when he was a little boy! Yes sir, them Winters genes is strong! Lil' old cute self. Just as fat as he could be!

After a few weeks or so, Robin and I got to talking again and we decided to go 'head and surprise Lauren with the baby shower. Greg told me that they was taking the baby to the pediatrician on that particular day so, knowing they'd probably be gone for a while, I told Robin, we both told the family and we got to work putting it all together.

A nice, pretty green tablecloth was draped across a round table full of cupcakes, cookies, candy and presents. Anything you could think of. Robin said she didn't really care for that color green but I thought it went good with the nursery so we stuck with it. I ain't much of a fashion nova but I do alright.

So, Nate and Gina hung up the banner while Robin wrapped a big old green bow around a single chair. Just one chair - for Lauren to sit in. That was her day! Now, I don't do too much meddling in other folks' business but I don't know why in the hell Nate thought he could pull a wool over my eyes! I knew him and Gina had been messing around outside of wedlock! Them boys don't never think I got my own life to tend to but I do. I'm back on the market, you know? And I sure don't got time to give a damn about who they laying up with. But I knew it. Sure did! I knew it! Runnin' around the house giggling and all that petting. I knew it. Yes, I did. Yes, I did! I called it.

It was just a few of us gathering over at the house for the baby shower - me and Robin, Kenneth came - that's her daddy. A couple of Lauren's lil' friends showed up; I don't know their names. Nate and Gina and uh, Lauren's granddaddy - they called him PawPaw. He sure was funny to me. He really was. Just walking around the house, sipping and snacking on everything he could get his hands on. He and Lauren was real, real close before he passed. They was. I hear she was close to her grandmother, too but she passed before I got a chance to meet her. That's the one they named Lauren after - her middle name, rather. Ivory. That's pretty, ain't it? *Ivory…*

Anyhow, I was in the dining room mixing up the punch and Kenneth stood over by the big window in the front, looking outside, just watching and waiting for Greg 'nem to pull in the driveway. He nearly ate up *all* the cookies, too! And I don't know which doctor they took the baby to see but Lord, it took them a long time to make it home. Must've drove to Tuscaloosa, all that time passed! Another hour or so went by before they got home but we had *been* ready for 'em.

"Alright, they're here!" Kenneth yelled out while he stuffed that last cookie down his throat.

We wasn't *trying* to be in they business, you see, but we all just kinda looked at 'em through the window, you know. I was so proud of my son, watching him be a gentleman and look after his wife the way he did. He stood in the passenger side door while Lauren wrapped her arms around his neck. I could tell she wasn't fully healed yet because she took a deep breath and winced as Greg helped her stand to her feet. She was hurtin'. I knew she was. I had two children of my own, remember? I know how it feels.

Greg gently pulled her forward and closed the car door behind her as he reached down and grabbed lil' Greg's carseat from the ground. Now, I wouldn't have had my newborn *or* my new carseat sitting on that concrete, but these young folks is different. And you know, I could tell something wasn't right before that girl went in that house because of how she looked up and sort of glared at the house as they approached it. Naw, buddy. Something was *off*! But, I didn't say nothing at the time because I didn't wanna upset her and I just figured she'd get over whatever it was soon enough.

Did they know we was in they house? Naw! We was trying to surprise 'em, fool! Anyhow, soon as we heard that key hit the door, I snatched my apron off, chucked it under the table and smacked my lips together while I touched up my lipstick. I looked in my pocketbook and all I had with me was my dark red so I put it on. I didn't think nothin' of it at first, but later on, I caught a glimpse of my reflection through the window and there I was, looking like a damn floozy at the baby shower! Lord, have mercy!

Robin fluffed up her hair, Nate palm-checked his breath and Gina fixed her dress. It was a good-looking dress, too. Fit her real nice. Yes, honey. Gina got a shape on her and apparently, Nate thought so, too, if you know what I mean. So, we all hurried and gathered in front of the table and started posing and here come Gina and her silly ass, busting out laughing!

Talking about, "Okay, I'm sorry. I just don't know why we're posing."

Hell, I didn't know either, but I didn't say nothing.

So, I just told everybody to hush and then Nate's mannish tail gon' call out, "Ma?" like I didn't just tell his ass to hush!

And of course, Gina started giggling again and Nate went to talkin' 'bout, "Shut up, I had a question."

I'll tell you, these kids, they grow up and get too grown for their own britches. Alright, I gotta get back to my cornbread directly, so let me just get to the point. So, Greg and Lauren and the baby, they come on in the house and we started cheering 'em on. Clapping and shouting out, and carrying on.

"First of all," Greg asked, "how did all of y'all get in my house?"

You should've seen his face!

"Now, you know good and well," I told him," I can get in any house I wanna get in!"

He knew it, too. Mama come from the old school!

Everybody started laughing and the whole time, Lauren was just standing around, looking… almost like she hadn't never been there, or maybe like she didn't even know who none of us was. I knew she did but she didn't look like she did. All of a sudden, it got real quiet and awkward-like in the house. Robin cleared her throat and smiled as she eagerly approached Lauren.

"Hi, sweetheart! You look gorgeous!" she said.

She did, too. She looked real nice. Real pretty, the way she had her hair pin't up. And I liked that sundress she had on, too. Looked real good on her. Burgundy, I think it was. And she didn't have no type of belly. She looked good, she did. I could tell that Robin knew something was up with her, though, but she didn't say nothin'. And I thought for sure that Gina would be able to perk her up.

"Hey girl!!! I see your boobs came back," she told her. "Heyyyy!"

But Lauren just looked down at her bosom, then looked back up at Gina. It was strange! It was sure strange. I think all of us could tell that Lauren just wasn't behaving like the Lauren we all knew, but I think Kenneth was the most concerned about her at the time. Every time I looked over at him, he had his eyes all narrow, just watching her like a hawk.

So, I jabbed Nate on the arm then he rushed over and kissed

Lauren on the cheek.

"You look good, sis," he told her.

He's real sweet, when he wants to be. Anyhow, Nate took the carseat out of Greg's hand and took the baby over to the couch and sat down with him for a while. It just got real odd in the room. The whole energy was just odd. Greg kept grinning, even when it wasn't nothin' to be grinning 'bout. It was a mess.

"Well, don't just stand there," I told 'em. "Y'all come in and get settled. I baked cookies, and Lauren honey, your mama made some… Uh…"

Hell, I couldn't even think straight with all that awkwardness! I know my son and I could tell he was trying to make Lauren loosen up a little.

"Come on, baby. You hungry?" That's what he said. "Want me to make you a plate? Lauren?" But, she didn't say nothin'. Now, that wasn't like her at all. Long as I had known Lauren, she was just as friendly and welcoming. Lord, Jesus. She was always 'bout her business but she enjoyed being around her people any chance she got.

So, we all started getting settled, checking on the baby and trying to enjoy the shower when all of a sudden, Lauren put on this *ghostly* smile. Honey, child!

"Thanks everybody," she said. "This is nice. I'm just gonna go lie down for a while, if that's alright," she told us.

I didn't mind it but the whole reason we was there in the first place was for her. We all started lookin' around and Gina went over and tried to find out what was wrong with her.

"I'm just tired," that's all she said.

She was tired. Us mothers, we understood *tired* so Robin just told her that it was fine and to go on and get some rest. Kenneth quietly observed her as she walked right on past him and headed toward the stairwell.

"Just give her some time," Robin told everybody. "She'll come around."

And that's what we all was hoping for, you know what I mean? Lauren went on up the stairs and I went to fix me a plate so all that good food wouldn't go to waste. And just as soon as I turned around, here come PawPaw, chomping down on some damn cashews.

"Told y'all she wasn't gonna like this shit," he said. "It's tacky, if you ask me. Should'a went with brown. Everybody like brown," he carried on.

I don't care for brown, myself, but I did cackle. He sure was funny, bless his heart. Yes, he was.

* * *

I wasn't really in the mood to see anyone. I hadn't slept more than two hours at a time since Gregory was born. I was exhausted. My breasts felt like sacks of potatoes, and I really couldn't take the chance that someone would catch me crying because I knew that they would ask me what was wrong. And I didn't have a decent answer for anyone, not even for myself.

Some days, I would hold Gregory in my arms and I just couldn't imagine my life without him. But those days were few and far in between and they had started to feel nonexistent. I cried over everything and I felt increasingly guilty because I wasn't the happy, grateful mother I always believed I would be. I kept him fed. I kept him clean. I kept him safe. And I don't think I had anything more than that to give.

Every now and again, I would have an urge to finish writing the novel I started, but I felt crippled and found it more and more difficult to focus long enough to follow through. My book tour ended abruptly when I went into labor and even though I had always planned to return to my career, for some reason, *I couldn't.*

I felt as though Gregory deserved a better mother, better than my mind had convinced me that I could ever be. One that didn't question her love for him. One that always *wanted* to hold him. Because I wasn't always sure what I was feeling... or seeing. And I might as well be completely honest with you - after a while, I only held him because he would cry endlessly if I didn't, and I hated that. Even though I was surrounded by love, I felt completely alone for the first time in my entire life. Not lonely like I'd often felt as a young child or when Holly's absence followed me around. I felt *alone* - emotionally and mentally isolated from everyone - including myself, as strange as that sounds to confess. But I didn't tell anyone that I was struggling, at least not at first. Who was I going to tell? Who would even understand what I was going through if I didn't understand it myself?

I remember one night, I was downstairs, alone —either in the kitchen or the living room— I'm not exactly sure at the moment. I was so tired and it was storming heavily. Angry raindrops were beating against the windows and the roof as thunder violently shook the night sky. Suddenly, I could feel this... this sort of demonic darkness in the house and I felt like it was slowly luring me from downstairs up. The wild wind whistled and I could hear a gentle jingling sound in the distance, so I followed it upstairs.

Darkness steadily pulled me down the hallway and as the jingle grew nearer, soft voices and a small light escaped a room in the corner. I grew curious and decided to take a look inside.

I entered and walked over to this oversized crib in the center of the room. I was so out of it that at first, I didn't even realize that I was standing in the nursery and that Gregory's big brown eyes were bulging back at mine. And the jingle, it was just his musical mobile hovering overhead.

But would you like to know what was even more bizarre about that night? It never even happened. I hadn't walked up the stairs. There hadn't been any supernatural forces luring me into that room. I had been standing in that nursery, *dreaming* the entire time! My eyes popped open and Gregory's earth-shattering scream shook me out of it, but when I discovered what was happening, my hand was pressed down over his little mouth. His scream was a cry for help… for me, just as much as it was for himself.

"How had I gotten to that place?" I wondered.

Even my reaction to what I now knew was delayed. As he laid there gasping for air, a single tear fell from my eyes down onto his small and helpless face.

"Oh, dear God," I suddenly thought to myself, though not sudden enough, as I *finally* removed my hand from over his mouth.

Fully aware in that moment, I quickly picked him up out of his crib and cradled him in my arms. My poor baby was so scared! It took a while for him to fully relax but he eventually settled down. I stroked his head and rubbed his back as I turned around and walked over to my wooden rocker. It was the same one my mother used when I was a baby… the same one my grandmother used for my mother, and for relaxation when long days had gotten the best of her.

"Mommy's so sorry," I told him as I began to hum the words to a song I could hardly even remember anymore.

But even in the midst of my admission, I didn't *feel* sorry. At least not in the way one might expect, you know – sorry for scaring him or for not knowing any better, perhaps. I felt sorry because the honest version of myself would have never entrusted my baby to a stranger, and I was afraid that a stranger was all I had to offer him.

After a few minutes, I looked up and saw Greg watching me from the doorway. He looked worried as I wiped my wet eyes with the back of my hand, tilted my head at him and smiled in effort to convince him that all was well. Gregory's chilling scream had awakened him and little did I know that a character that I didn't even create had awakened inside of me.

10

The Character

Harvey David Winters was a special type of man. He not only took good care of his wife and kids, he also took care of all the people in our neighborhood who, for some reason or another, couldn't take care of themselves. When he grilled out on Friday nights, he would invite everybody on Dorsey Street to stop by and have a bite to eat, and the only person that ever turned him down was Miss Maddie - the old Southern sweetheart on our street who couldn't stand big crowds, fast-tailed lil' girls and folks breathing over her food. But that didn't stop her from devouring every crumb on the plate that I personally delivered to her every Friday just before the others arrived.

"Who made the macaroni?" she would ask me *every single time* as I pulled out her wooden tray and got her set up for dinner.

When my father shopped for me and Nate, he shopped for our friends whose fathers either couldn't or wouldn't do it for them. He kept an open heart, and in his mind, strangers were just people he hadn't introduced himself to yet. He was a natural provider, a lover without hesitation and he felt like the most important thing he could do was drive me to school every morning. He wanted to talk to me. He wanted to get inside of my head to understand where I stood on life, and he wanted to lead me to believe that limits didn't exist. And they don't.

"What's on your mind, son?" he would ask like clockwork when we would pull up to the light on 2nd Avenue.

"Nothing," I would always reply, but I knew that he wasn't having that.

"Fill your mind with shit other folks wouldn't understand son, and you'll wind up dreaming about shit that most folks didn't know was an option," he would say.

And that's what we did. He would buy me books about Sasquatch and American conspiracy theories, take me on Black History tours of towns big and small and he would teach me about money - how to make it, how to spend it and how to make some more. He taught me about ownership and showed me what a confident Black dreamer looked like. And he never let me settle for shit that didn't move me. So, I didn't.

Rest Miss Maddie's soul and rest my daddy's.

I was pretty young when my father passed away, but I understood that I was next in line to look after my mama and my little brother, at least that was the kind of pressure that I felt. So, even though I did my thing and had fun, I was careful not to do anything too stupid because I never wanted to risk them not having me around. As soon as I was old enough to get a work permit, I went and got myself a job selling vacuum cleaners door-to-door around the county. I hated that shit, too, but I was good at it and the money was decent enough that I could help my mama put food on the table and buy my brother new shoes from time to time. I wanted to be responsible, I wanted to step into my father's shoes and I wanted to show everybody that I could handle whatever needed to be handled. But my mama was stubborn as hell. She still is. So, our plans… collided, if you will.

"Boy, I don't want that shit!" she'd tell me whenever I would come home with bags full of groceries. "March your narrow behind right on back down there to that store, give it all back to 'em and take that money upstairs to that piggy bank your aunt Doreen bought you for Christmas. I can handle *my* house," she'd always say.

I love my mama, man. I just think that my dad's death forced me to grow up faster than most people I knew. In my mind, I had become a man. And the man that I was a product of showed up for the people he loved. So, I kept coming home with groceries. Kept taking plates to Miss Maddie until she died. Kept bringing Jordan's home for Nate. And I kept taking it all back to the store, stuffing that piggy bank while unknowingly being groomed to be the real man both of my parents dreamed I would become, and not a minute sooner than I needed to.

My mama would tell me, "It ain't time for all of that yet, Greg. Just be my son."

She didn't want my dad's death to deprive me of my childhood and I believed that she thought she knew what was best for me. And for the most part, she did. But, there were limits and some things were just unavoidable. And even though my mama meant well, I had learned lessons from my father that just made more sense to me as a young, Black boy. I think she understood that, but my father was no longer around to soften the blow when my testosterone threatened her authority.

Growing up, I think everybody kind of looked at me like I

was a big brother. Not just to Nate, you know? Even to guys my own age, in school or whatever type of thing I was involved in at the time. Sports… basketball, track, tennis. I pretty much played everything. I was in all different types of school clubs, you know. But it wasn't just guys; it was girls, too. Some of everybody. They all looked up to me for whatever reason. I always just talked to people, listened to their problems and I gave them advice when they asked me to. And they *always* asked. I just tried to be a good friend, and even if my mama wasn't willing to let me be the man of the house just yet, in my social circles, I was naturally *that* guy.

I had been working for about two years when this dude, Marcus, got hired and we was basically friends from his first day. He was about a year older than me but we had a lot in common. His dad died when he was little and he was the oldest child, too. Both of our moms did hair on the side and we both liked cream soda on our lunch breaks. We were similar, Marcus and me. I think that's why we got along so well. You know, I was good at selling vacuums but Marcus and the energy that he had… man, there wasn't a person he came in contact with that didn't walk away believing that they *needed* a new vacuum cleaner. The only time he *didn't* sell vacuums was on his off days, and even then, people would be calling the warehouse looking for him. It was pretty wild but Marcus made a lot of money.

One evening after work, Marcus had invited me to go to a house party with him. He told me that his parents were out of town and that he and his sister were inviting some friends over for fun and games that Saturday night. I was seventeen at the time and I know this might sound crazy, but I wasn't really all that into parties back then. Don't get me wrong, I did do stuff for fun, like bowling or going to the movies and shit like that.

But aside from the backyard cookouts my father used to throw, I've never been one for big crowds of people, especially people that I don't know but I *did* know Marcus. I've always loved people but being stuffed up inside of a house with loud music and hormones in the Georgia heat just wasn't me. But aside from choppin' it up on the job, Marcus and I hadn't really hung out outside of work, so when he invited me to the party, I told him I'd go.

So, I get to the party. I was wearing my Dallas Cowboys jersey, jeans, my cap backwards, my chain… I was real clean. And the first thing I did was poured myself a drink… ginger ale and cranberry juice. Because for one, Evelyn Winters would have killed my ass if I had even *thought* about coming home drunk after she trusted me to go to the party in the first place. And for two, I didn't feel like explaining to people why I wasn't drinking. I'm grown now, so I don't mind it but back then, I just wanted to sip my soda in peace.

The music was bumping, everybody was having a good time and I had been held hostage in a corner by a brokenhearted Bobby Walker who felt the need to justify to *me* why he had started stalking his ex-girlfriend, Kujuanna, when she stopped answering his calls. Bobby didn't know me and I didn't know Kujuanna but like I told you before, I was like everybody's big brother. I had refilled my drink so much that I found myself running to the bathroom at least twice every hour and every time I came out, Bobby was right outside that door, smiling and waiting to tell me more.

But one time, I was walking out of the bathroom and the most beautiful girl I had ever seen was waiting outside the door.

She had the prettiest brown skin and back then, Black girls weren't really wearing their hair natural, but she was. It looked good on her, too and she knew it. That was the best part. The sweet smell of cocoa butter and caramel swept me off of my feet and I must have stood in the doorway of that bathroom for a whole two minutes, just captivated. I was lost.

"Excuse me," she said in her cute little raspy voice. "Are you finished in there?"

"Oh, my bad," I told her. "Yeah, it's all yours."

I might have been finished using the bathroom, at least for the time being, but I wasn't finished with her and I for damn sure wasn't leaving that party without her number. I didn't want to come off as a weirdo, so I let Bobby finish his long-ass story then I moved around the party like I had been doing before his breakdown took over. And when I wasn't moving around, I would just be chillin' when I felt the urge. But you better believe that my eyes were searching for that girl and after a couple of hours of not crossing paths with her, I prepared myself for the possibility that she had left. But when I stepped outside for a minute to get some fresh air, there she was, sitting on the steps, apparently with the same thing in mind. So, I sat down next to her and did my best to play it cool.

"I've been looking for you," I boldly confessed, sounding and behaving like my father used to sound when he found himself missing my mama after a long day of her rippin' and runnin'.

"What?" she replied, her eyebrows furrowed and five seconds away from going back inside the house.

"I said I've been looking for you," I repeated as I looked her directly in the eyes. "I love your hair, I think you're pretty and I was hoping that we could talk some more."

"Some more?" she asked, pretending not to remember me

from the doorway.

So then I was like, "So, you're telling me that we locked eyes for at least two minutes outside of that bathroom and you don't remember me?"

She pressed her lips together, rolled her eyes and with the slightest grin on her face, she turned her head away.

"I remember you," she said, all nonchalantly.

"So, what's your name?" I asked her.

"I'm Lauren," she said. "Lauren Ivory Ellis."

I liked her name, the way her top lip curled upwards when she smiled and the way her delicate hands would hold both sides of her face when she was really into the conversation. She was everything I could have ever dreamed of in a girl and I wanted to know everything there was to know about her. We spent the rest of that night talking on those steps. We swapped stories from our adolescence, memories our mothers gave us and we shared dreams of one day growing into the people we ultimately became. Her confidence was even more beautiful than her face and her mind was more appealing than either of them.

I may have been young but I was in love… And yes, my mama kicked my *ass* when I walked up in her house at six o'clock the next morning! But man, I took that ass whoopin' like a champ because as far as I was concerned, I had already won. Lauren was the woman of my dreams, and I was so distracted by my thoughts that I didn't feel any of it, anyway. It really just wore my mama's shoulders out.

Lauren had gotten lucky, though, because it was her cousin, Denise's party and she was spending the night with her while Denise's parents were out of town. And you probably already put it together, but Marcus was Denise's older brother. If it wasn't for him, I don't know if Lauren and I would have ever met. I told him that every chance I got, too. That was my boy; I miss him. He was killed in a motorcycle accident a few years back.

But yeah, Lauren and I got real close and that was pretty much how it had been for the majority of our relationship… the both of us, so madly in love with one another that nothing could destroy us. But after Gregory was born, shit was… just different. I knew that Lauren was having a hard time adjusting to being a mom and I knew she was tired and probably missing her old life. I understood. But everything revolved around Gregory and after I returned to work, it was just the two of them at the house most of the time. I know that had to be hard but at that time, I couldn't just leave my business to run itself. So, I had to do what I had to do. And I blame myself for not being around more. Maybe I could have stopped things from getting so out of control. No way to know now, I guess.

I'm sure that I missed a few red flags but the first thing that really struck me as odd was how Lauren would turn into this… almost like this vixen or some shit. She had gotten really protective of Gregory and she started getting more and more worried that if she didn't protect him, something bad might happen. Of course, I wanted to keep my family safe, too, you know, so whenever she was feeling paranoid about something, I would just do whatever needed to be done for her to feel comfortable. She wanted new locks on all the doors, so I installed new locks. She didn't think the baby monitors were good enough, so we got new ones. And when she told me that she might feel safer if the house was fenced in, I made some calls and got a few estimates. Later on, she changed her mind but I did try to make her happy.

So, this one particular time —it was the middle of the night—she was in the nursery feeding the baby for like the fifth time that night. She was exhausted and I got up to check on her after she had been in there for a long time. I was standing in the doorway when all of a sudden, I hear this loud, buzzing sound. The whole house went black and all I could see was Lauren's eyes. She looked scared as hell. And I can't lie, I was a little scared, too.

I went and grabbed the flashlight out of my nightstand drawer and started checking around the house to see if I could figure out what the issue was. I checked the fuse box to see if the lights would come back on. Nothing. I searched all the rooms, but everything looked good so I went outside and took a look around out there. Turned out, the whole neighborhood had lost power.

Now, I never really felt the way Lauren felt about cats, but I would be lying if I said I wasn't creeped the fuck out when I turned around out there and saw a whole flock of them mothafuckas just sitting in the front yard looking at me! Can you imagine that? It's pitch black outside and all I see is cat eyes. But shit got even creepier when I got back inside, though.

I walked back past the nursery and didn't see Lauren. So, I walked down to our bedroom and there she was in this sexy, red lingerie. Not to really put our business out there like that, but we hadn't had sex in a while. And even when we did, we were so comfortable with each other's naked bodies that we really didn't do the whole lingerie thing. So, it was weird to see. Then there was the whole glow from this large, burning candle, just shining on her face… and a bottle of champagne on ice, which was odd because Lauren didn't really drink like that. Her red lips imprinted her glass as she lowered it from her lips, placed it on her nightstand and smiled at me.

"Wanna play?" she asked me in a kinda sultry, Latin accent.

Now, that shit had me all fucked up. Lauren didn't talk like that! Like… like role playing and shit. Nah, not Lauren. And don't even ask me how she pulled all of it together that fast in the dark because I still can't make sense of it. But she was all dressed up and I didn't wanna make her feel bad or hurt her feelings, so I just made my way over to my side of the bed and smiled back at her.

"Baby, what's all this?" I asked, completely confused.

As I sat down, she crawled up behind me and ran her fingers up and down my spine. She kissed my neck as she moved around from my back onto my lap, swung her legs tightly around my waist, slid her robe off and pressed her bare breasts into my chest.

"I want you," she whispered in my ear.

My breath deepened as her kisses became licks, her licks became sucks and as weirded out as I felt, it had been a *long* time since we had been that close and I wanted her, too.

"Lauren?" I said as I tried to get some control over the situation.

But the further down my body she explored, the harder it was to resist her.

"Lauren, stop," I said, still trying.

"And I know what you really want," she whispered again.

It was as if her eyes were smiling at me. She was teasing me and slowly but surely, she slid my "you know what" down her throat. I relaxed my head as I guided hers to the right spot. But as much as it *felt* like my wife, she behaved like a character from a story I wasn't too familiar with. Little did I know, there was an entire crew of characters just waiting to tell their sides of the story.

11

The Crew

There were certain negative notions that people often connected to our culture that my mother outright refused to subscribe to. In our home, we didn't reuse cooking oil, we didn't use the word "nappy", we didn't cover our clean couches with plastic and if the plan was to ever go *anywhere*, we were to arrive on time or not at all. And I use the term *we* because if you lived under my mother's roof, you followed my mother's rules.

"Tardiness is tacky," she would say as she hurried me out of the house and into the school building fifteen minutes before the first bell rang every single day.

I wasn't going to be late for *my* obligations and she refused to be late for hers, fooling around with me. My mother was prompt and everyone who knew her had come to expect that from her. Some people didn't like her and some said that she thought she was better than other people. But those who really took the time to watch and observe her really appreciated being in her presence.

Yes, she will always be a free-spirited creative who fancies fabrics and florals, fairy-tale fantasies and frilly formals. However, my mother is equally talented in business management, organization and the execution of whatever needs to be executed… talents that made her successful in her own life and talents that strongly influenced the trajectory of mine. She raised me to be conscious, aware and in tune with myself, and I have tried my best to remain true to those values that have since grown to become my own.

For a very long time, the attention I placed on even the tiniest details of my life produced every result that I desired. I was determined to be a successful writer so I wrote daily for more than two decades. Having a clean home was a priority for me, so I vowed to never go to bed with dishes in my sink or dirt on my floor. And growing up with happily married parents whose love for me was never in doubt left no questions in my mind about wanting the same for myself. I knew exactly what I wanted out of life and I never believed in wasting time on distractions that didn't drive me in the direction of those things. And that included romantic relationships.

My father *kept* my mother laughing. He believed in her just as much as he believed in himself. He refused to bury chivalry. And he showed her the respect that he believed was owed to *all* Black women in this country. I *knew* my mother was happy and I was unwilling to settle for anything less than the example my father had set for me.

"The *real* women who made America," he would always refer to them as, and later on me, when my mother caught a spell of the creative waves and required a boost of confidence.

Greg and I met when we were both just seventeen years old. Of course I thought he was cute ,but even then, I was more interested in what was on the inside than what my eyes could see. Now, don't get me wrong - looks *are* important to me. But Greg was very confident and direct, which I loved even from our first conversation, which lasted all night long, by the way. And before your imagination gets the best of you, no, it was not that type of night. He was a gentleman, and I felt no pressure to perform beyond the borders of conversation. We just talked as we fell madly in love under the stars.

Besides my mother, I had been the only person I knew who had dreams as big as mine. Dreams that reached far past America's white picket fences. Dreams in which boundaries and impossibilities were nonexistent. And dreams that most people suppressed for fear of failing only to wake up years later and find themselves failing at freedom. I had *big* dreams but Greg's dreams stretched my mind in directions I never knew existed. That's what I love the most about him.

We dated for *years* before we decided to marry. And despite persistent pressure from our peers and relatives to make it official, we agreed to honor *our* needs and to allow time and experiences to secure our foundation. We had both witnessed the rise and fall of many young marriages made prematurely - something we didn't want for ourselves. So, we took our time, maintained a long-distance relationship throughout college and moved in together right after graduation in an effort to get accustomed to functioning in the same space - which naturally came with its own set of challenges.

Greg wasn't necessarily a slob but it would drive me crazy when I would find his worn socks stuffed between the cushions of our couches. Wherever he undressed, his dirty clothes called their home. And his idea of cleaning the kitchen consisted of piling the dishes into the dishwasher and sweeping the floor. Okay, fine... he *was* a slob. And I didn't want to turn into that girlfriend that nitpicked her boyfriend's every move, but I had grown up in a pristine environment that *always* smelled like a breath of fresh air, so living in filth and having to smell stinky socks was not something I was comfortable with. But as time passed, Greg's cleanliness improved, I relaxed my guard a little and we were able to move past that... just not in the kitchen. He still sucked very badly in the kitchen! Oh, the bathroom, too. But, we managed to make things work.

Forgive me if I seem a bit scattered but preparing to talk about these things isn't easy for me. I would rather focus on the good days and all the love we made. But I know that's not enough and I need you to understand how I got here. Alright? I wasn't always this way and I do have a story beyond what you've read about me.

You know, losing Holly disrupted my process but having Gregory really dismantled me. As I struggled to survive the frequent feedings, nonstop neediness and the voices of insufficiency inside my head, the values my mother had instilled in me many years ago —the values in which I lived by— had suddenly vanished. And with the emotional and mental drainage of my increasingly powerful paranoia, unnerving nightmares *or* dreams from the day, and a series of events seemingly perpetrated by no one, I no longer had the energy or desire to exist in ways I'd grown accustomed to. I suppose that's when the trouble really began. In fact, I'm quite embarrassed to admit that I still remember the first time I begged Greg to call the police.

"Okay, let's try this again," the officer said in a tone filled with doubt and discrimination. "Did you actually see someone in your home?" he asked.

We hadn't.

"Is there any evidence of a forced entry?" he asked.

And there wasn't.

But no one could have told me otherwise during that time. As I sat there holding Gregory while this middle-aged, heavyset, heavily unattractive police officer insulted us and chalked up our experience to parental forgetfulness, I found it difficult to hold back my tears. I *knew* what I had seen… what I had felt. No, I couldn't quite prove it but I believed that we were in *real* danger and if the authorities weren't willing to help us, who was?

Earlier that night, Greg and I were in bed. He was asleep and I just remember lying there with my eyes shut, hoping to fall back to sleep before Gregory's next feeding. I don't recall exactly what time it was but I do know that it was sometime after 3am. It was still very dark outside, I do know that. So, we were lying in bed together and out of nowhere, this wave of wind swept through our bedroom and sent objects flying *everywhere*. I clenched the comforter as the ceiling fan suddenly blew aggressively overhead and I just laid there, petrified for minutes before I built up enough courage to finally sit up. Meanwhile, Greg snoozed, seemingly unbothered.

Our curtains clung to the window ledges as a thick layer of frost covered them. Unidentified documents flew about the room. And my robe, which I conveniently kept at the foot of our bed was soaking wet. I *knew*… I could just *feel* that someone was in the house. I knew it. I could smell it. As I quietly shook Greg to wake him, I worried that whoever had done this had either taken Gregory or was in the process of doing something awful to us. And even though I knew that I needed to rescue him or… or somehow save *us* from whatever was out there, I was too terrified to *do* anything. In total transparency, a darker part of me didn't want to.

"Greg, wake up!" I whispered as my head twitched around the room in response to what I was seeing.

"What is it?" he asked as he squinted then rubbed his eyes open. "What's wrong?"

"Look," I uttered as I nodded in the direction of the disaster before us. "Somebody's in the house," I said, sure of it.

"Please," I begged him. "*Do* something."

* * *

I was more worried about Lauren than I was about somebody being in the house that night. Yeah, the house had gotten a little messy in the days since Gregory was born, and yeah, it was a little chilly that night. I mean, it *was* November and despite what people believe, it does get cold in Georgia. But when she woke me up, shaking and paranoid and shit, I really just went to check out the house to ease her mind, you know? I thought she may have been having a nightmare but she was *convinced* that we were under some kind of attack.

The first thing I did was turn the heat up. I made sure all the windows were closed and locked. I checked on the baby and then I made my way around the rest of the house to double-check that everything else was secure. It was all good but again, I wasn't worried anyway. But Lauren wasn't satisfied and she insisted that I call the cops. So, against my better judgment, I called them.

The officer asked if we had reviewed the footage from our home security system, which reminded me that I never got around to replacing the damn tape like Lauren had asked me to while she was pregnant. And as I stood there listening to this dude explain that we lacked sufficient evidence to build a case, the fear in Lauren's eyes told me that something was definitely wrong. I held her in my arms for the rest of the night and she laid there, staring at Gregory, who was now in his bassinet next to our bed. Lauren was deathly afraid of something. I don't even know if she knew what that was.

A couple of days later, I walked out to my car. It was morning and I was getting ready to leave for work. It was a beautiful day, too. There was this radiant rainbow, a bright blue sky, and the trees were blowing gently in the wind. And it was sunny. It was cold as hell but it was nice. Lauren had finally gotten a little sleep the night before. We talked and she admitted that maybe she *had* had a bad dream after all. As far as I could tell, her mind was at ease, so I felt pretty comfortable returning to work after what had happened that weekend.

As I approached my car, I could hear what sounded like ice being crushed under my shoes. I looked down to find glass glistening all over the concrete then looked forward to find that all of the windows in my brand-new luxury sedan had been shattered and this ugly-ass silver lining surrounded the entire exterior of the car. I was livid!

"So, you have no idea who would have done this to you?" the investigating officer asked me for the third time.

"I already said that," I replied, irritated with the interrogation and frustrated with the facts.

This time when the office asked about surveillance footage, I felt better knowing that I had finally replaced that tape. But I felt completely defeated when we went upstairs to review the footage and were met with a disconnected surveillance system. I didn't understand. I had no reason to unplug the surveillance system. I wouldn't do that and it didn't make sense to me.

"I must have mistakenly disconnected it before I went to bed last night," I explained to the officer.

But I knew that I hadn't really done that. And as Lauren sat there, oddly quiet… almost as if she was shy or something, I didn't want to admit my suspicions but I couldn't help but wonder if this was somehow connected to what had happened the other night. I couldn't prove it and I didn't want to upset Lauren by questioning her or accusing her of anything. All I really knew was that my dream car had been destroyed in my own driveway and the officer on the scene hadn't believed a word I said to him. But in the back of my mind, I did wonder.

* * *

The way I saw it, if Greg wasn't willing to take things seriously, I had no choice but to take matters into my own hands. I wasn't going to sit around and hope for the best. I wasn't going to pray that things got better. And I wasn't going to be made to feel crazy all because these people couldn't understand my raging passion to protect us. So, after the officer left, I called Regional Home Security and demanded that they come out and replace our surveillance system —the only part of the house that hadn't been replaced before we moved in— with something a little less dated. I'll admit that I should have mentioned it to Greg before I made my decision, but I didn't feel like we had any more time to waste. But Greg sure as hell wasn't okay with it.

"What's there to talk about?" I bitterly replied when he asked why I hadn't discussed it with him beforehand.

I was on a mission to catch whoever the hell this criminal was and I wasn't going to stand by and watch everything we had worked so hard for get snatched away from us! At least that was the level of passion I possessed on some days. On other days, I fell victim to the sofa, endlessly watching the news reports, hoping to receive answers to the mysteries that plagued me, all the while hearing sad stories of petty crimes that had taken over our neighborhood. I was tired. Life felt complicated. And in the midst of my panic, I had, unbeknownst to me, picked up a bit of a habit.

"I know that smell!" my father announced when he showed up at our house unannounced one afternoon.

"What smell?" I asked.

"That's a Montecristo… Number 4, baby girl! Top shelf!" he explained. "I didn't know Greg liked cigars," he said.

Because he didn't. And last I had checked, neither did I. But when a rummage through every drawer in the house brought me to the top of my very own nightstand, I felt confused and disconnected from myself as I pulled out a lighter, lit the partially consumed cigar, gave in to the sudden and strong urge and finished it off like a pro. As I sat at the edge of my bed exhaling smoke into the air, I felt an overwhelming sense of detachment from my body. It felt like I was watching myself do things I would never do and in that moment, I wanted nothing more than to kill my husband. The longer I sat, the more powerful the desire felt. It's so difficult for me to say this out loud but sitting there … I *hated* Greg.

Feeling completely disgusted with myself for ever letting Greg come near me, I decided to take a shower in an effort to wash off any trace of him. I couldn't scrub hard enough and my mind raced with plans to punish him for whatever he had done to me. But when the shower turned off, my feelings of resentment were replaced with laughter that I had no explanation for. As my wet feet stepped down onto the cool floor, I felt like I was watching a performance in which I was unknowingly cast as the star.

As I wiped the fog from the bathroom mirror with my hand, I slowly revealed my reflection. I furrowed my eyebrows as I realized that the face in the mirror had its own agenda. My curiosity grew as the face mocked my every motion. As I tilted my head to the left, the strangely familiar face tilted its head to the right, grinning back at me. And as I turned around to see who this person was, I was greeted with Luciferic laughter that sent chills running through my veins.

I nearly lost my mind trying to wipe the rest of the fog away. I was determined to stop whatever the hell was happening when suddenly, an angry scream startled me as it pushed through the nearby baby monitor. I jumped and as the scream quickly settled into a cry for food, I collected my breath and cautiously returned my gaze to the mirror. It wasn't over yet. The stranger chuckled, straightened her head and spoke with an accent I couldn't quite put my finger on.

"Pick your face up, bitch! It's only the baby," she told me.

In an instant rage, I balled up my fist and slammed it straight into the glass before I could even process what I was doing. As I stood there shaking uncontrollably, blood gushing from my fingers, I looked back up at the mirror and couldn't understand why it hadn't been shattered one bit. Confused, I looked back down at my hand and where blood once dripped, there *was* no blood. There was no pain, no evidence of a broken mirror or a busted fist. I was all alone. *I* was the stranger in the mirror. And I didn't know what to do with myself.

"Maybe you should see a counselor," Gina suggested when I told her I was having a hard time dealing with everything. But what I didn't tell her was that I had lost my mind and that an entire fucking crew of emotions living inside of me had gotten hold of it.

I had convinced myself that Gina wouldn't understand anyway. No one would. Not a single person on Earth would understand that I was quickly losing control over my own emotions, thoughts and actions. And even if someone did understand, my biggest fear was that I would be taken away from my family, locked inside of four walls that I couldn't escape and so far out of touch with reality that I wouldn't even notice. The irony though, was that I was already there.

<h1 style="text-align:center">12</h1>

<h1 style="text-align:center">The Counselor</h1>

You know what it's like when somebody has been a part of your life for so long that you hardly have any memories that don't include them? Well, that's us, Lauren and me. I won't tell you how old *I* am but I *will* say that Lauren and I have been friends since we were four years old - a *long* time. I was little but I'll never forget the day I met her. It was the first day of preschool and I was nervous because it was my first time being away from my family. I had never even gone to daycare or had a babysitter and the only other person that I had ever even spent the night with was my aunt Sharon. So, I was scared and awkward and I didn't really know what to do with myself.

On the ride in to school that morning, I remember my dad asking me what I wanted to eat for my first after-school dinner.

"It has to be special, GiGi," he said, "because you're special and this is a very special day."

I didn't feel very special and I could feel my heart pounding against my turtleneck. But a part of me was still excited because my dad had just told me that I could eat whatever I wanted to eat for dinner, so I thought about it for a few moments while I pretended not to smile.

"Tacos," I declared, fully aware that they were *his* favorite food.

"Tacos?!" he questioned.

"Yeah, tacos," I said. "With peanut butter and jelly, vanilla ice cream and sprinkles," I continued.

My dad laughed so hard and so long that I started laughing, too. I didn't know why he was laughing or why he couldn't stop but my dad's laughter was always so infectious that way. And he's still that same way, just a little bit older and a little bit senile but he's still a funny guy. Anyway, my dad and I were on the road, headed to Haley Street Elementary School - this big and intimidating brick building just a few miles or so from our house. As we pulled into the parking lot, my face must have given away my secret.

"When you walk into that school building, those teachers are going to wonder how they ever got along without you," my dad said as my laughter simmered down.

It was time. But my dad and I were late because he stopped to change the driver's side tire after he ran over a shredded tire on Mercury Road. I even got to help him and that was fun. I mean, I wasn't really that helpful, to be honest with you, but I at least got to watch… and get on his nerves a little.

"Don't you get no grease on that skirt, GiGi," he said as I handed him a tool he didn't ask me for. "You know your mama wouldn't like that."

He was right, she wouldn't have. And had she been alive, she probably would have styled my hair differently or made me wear stockings under my skirt or rubbed the back of my hand to help me relax. But bone cancer had taken her away from us a few months prior and as close as my dad and I were, he and I could both feel mom's absence that day.

When my dad walked me down to the attendance office, we were greeted by a young, edgy-looking secretary, Miss Neal. She had a short haircut and had three or four different color highlights in it. It was kinda like the girls wear now, with the bold colors that you don't really expect to see on somebody's head, only it's not as shocking because everybody's doing it. But Miss Neal's hair surprised the hell out of me because I had never seen anything like that in my young life before.

"Late already?" she asked as we stood in front of her, my eyes doing a terrible job at not focusing on her streaks.

My dad explained that he had stopped to change his tire and assured Miss Neal that I would be there bright and early Tuesday morning. And I was. But before I could get to Tuesday or the days that followed, I had to work my way through Monday.

"You must be Gina," our preschool teacher, Mrs. Peterson, smiled and said as I stood there shaking in the doorway.

I nodded my little head "yes," and she welcomed me into her primary color-filled classroom, packed with books, play sets and at least a dozen other kids my size.

"Put your book bag inside the cubby and find yourself a seat on the rug," she told me. But there were only two empty spaces - one next to this boy with crusty boogers all over his nose and mouth and another next to this girl who was wearing the prettiest purple dress I had ever seen before. Purple was my favorite color back then, so you know which one I chose. As I quietly took a seat next to her, I tripped over her shiny white patent leather Mary Jane's.

"Sorry," I whispered as I crossed my legs and settled in.

"It's okay," she said and as she smiled at me, I smiled back. "I'm Lauren Ivory Ellis," she said, all proud and shit. "Do you like cinnamon applesauce? My mommy put some in my lunchbox. We can share it, if you want."

And from that day on, Lauren and I shared everything! If I brought a hot dog to school for lunch, I gave her half. If she was wearing a pair of gloves and I was cold because I forgot mine at home, she would give me one of hers and we would hold our gloveless hands together to stay warm. And if anybody ever had any shit to talk about Lauren, I was more than happy to share a fist with them! Lauren was my homegirl and neither one of us was letting either one of us get fucked with. That's just how we were. Looking back, I'm glad that neither one of us actually ended up getting into a real fight because I really don't think either one of us could *actually* fight. Don't tell her I said that, though.

But anyway, it really messed me up when Lauren lost Holly. She and I had talked about becoming mothers since we were little girls. She always wanted her first baby to be a girl so that she could dress her up and do girl shit with her and even though neither of us had any control over any of it, I had agreed to have a girl first, too, so that they could be best friends and could play together just like me and Lauren. We had a plan and Lauren losing Holly meant that our plan had to change. We had grown up and understood life a lot more but it still hurt. I didn't really know what to do or how to make her feel better. So, I just listened to her when she was willing to talk and gave advice when she asked me for it. That's all I could do.

When her pregnancy with lil' Greg was confirmed, I was excited as hell though! Not only did I know that Lauren was gonna be an incredible mother, I just *knew* that I was gon' be an incredible aunt! Okay?! I hadn't had any kids of my own yet and none of my sisters or brothers had any at the time either, so I couldn't wait to spend my whole paycheck on that lil' boy. I bought so much shit that I still got half the shit folded up and stored in boxes inside my garage. Just throwing money away!

Anyway, I ended up feeling a little hurt after lil' Greg was born, though. I kept reaching out to Lauren, trying to get her to let me come over and see both of them but she didn't want any company. I offered to take her out to lunch at her favorite restaurant, to the art gallery, to Target… I just wanted to hang out with my best friend and have a chance to bond with the baby. And something about her voice on the phone and how she would switch topics and go from gloomy to glad about weird shit, I… Hell, I just needed to see what was going on with her for myself. I kept bugging her about it until she finally gave in and let me visit the house about a couple of months or so after the baby was born.

"I'm surprised you found enough lemons," she said as I joined her on the sofa with two glasses of freshly squeezed lemonade. "I haven't had a chance to go grocery shopping yet."

"Well, the ones I found *did* look a little old," I joked, "so if you get sick, you know why," I continued. "And don't you dare try to sue me because I'm not paying for shit! Don't come for me."

Seeing and hearing my friend laugh was exactly what I had been missing and I felt very grateful to be sitting there with her and her handsome baby boy, my nephew. But it didn't take me long to see that Lauren wasn't quite right.

"Damn, that's a lot of cats," I said to her as a furry feline family feasted over what looked like a pile of leftovers to me.

Lauren has *hated* cats her entire life so I was really confused when my comment was met with a smile.

I remember sitting there thinking, "Oh, hell no! What's really going on?"

I asked her if she was okay and at first, she said that she was fine. But the water in her eyes told a different story. I pressed my lips together as I placed my glass on the side table next to me. I knew that heffa had not just lied to my face like that, like I hadn't seen *every* expression she could possibly have!

"No, you're not," I disagreed. "What's wrong with you?"

She got real quiet for a minute then she closed her eyes and took a long, deep breath.

"Have you ever felt—" she started then stopped.

"Girl, felt what?" I impatiently asked.

"Weird, you know? Like you weren't quite yourself," she said. "Like… like your thoughts weren't your own or like your body belonged to someone else. Like you could do things, crazy things even, things you never even imagined. You ever felt like that, Gina?" she asked as she slowly turned her head and looked at me.

I told her that I hadn't. And after she shared a little bit more, I suggested she go see a counselor or a therapist. I thought it might help to talk to a professional.

"Girl no!" she laughed out as tears streamed down her face. "You know what? Nevermind. This lemonade is delicious! Isn't it?" she asked as she switched topics.

My stomach churned as she turned and smiled out the window. I sat there for the next couple of hours, holding lil' Greg and holding conversations with what felt like a total stranger. I should have pushed harder for her to go see somebody. I should've… I just wanted to be there for her, you know? So she would know that I still had her back no matter what. But, I feel so stupid and so guilty, even after all this time because I felt like, with the way Lauren and I were, I should have done more to help her! I should've done more. You know?

* * *

Lauren and I had small arguments from time to time, like any other couple. It was no big deal. But that night, I saw a side of her that I never imagined I would see. I had worked all day and I got in pretty late, took my shower and when I came into our bedroom, she just started going crazy on me. As I sat on the edge of the bed dressing myself, I struggled to get a single word in.

"I have had enough, Greg! *You* need to do something!" she asserted as she hovered over my body.

"Lauren, listen—" I began.

"No, you fucking listen!" she bullied as she pressed her index finger into my temple. "I am so sick and tired of you talking about what you're going to do to protect us. Somebody is trying to destroy this family right in front of you, bit by bit and every day you surprise me with how little you seem to give a damn!"

"Alright Lauren, chill," I said as I attempted to defend myself.

I mean… yeah somebody messing up my car was fucked up. Right? Having to explain to the cops that somebody neither of us heard or saw had broken into our house… that was fucked up, too. But did I think that somebody was out to *destroy* our family? No, I didn't.

So I just told her, "I think you're overreacting."

She started grinning as she got even closer to my face. It really pissed me off and I tried to stay calm but I honestly didn't know how much more I could take. She wouldn't listen to me and she just kept getting more and more angry - her eyes was bulging out of her head, veins popping out of her neck.

"I have sat by and watched and waited. Well, I'm tired of waiting!" she exclaimed.

"I don't know what you want from me, Lauren," I told her, not even really sure anymore if we were talking about the same thing. "I have done everything I can think of to keep this family safe!"

Then she lowered her face down to mine and stared me in the eyes with the coldest look I'd ever seen.

"Well, it isn't fucking good enough!" she said with this deep, emasculating voice.

As she stood there, enraged… almost like she was growling at me, I had had enough. I wanted to hear her out. I wanted to understand what she was going through, I really did. But I wasn't just going to sit there and let my wife treat me like I was a piece of shit. I stood to my feet, grabbed her arms and tossed her onto the bed.

"That's enough," I said as she laughed me off.

She quickly stood back up and started moving in close again and as much as I never wanted to raise my voice at her, in the heat of that moment, I didn't know what else to do to get my point across.

"I said that's enough!" I declared.

Just like that, rage and passion had separated us. And suddenly, out of nowhere, Lauren smiled and started taking her clothes off. Craziest shit I'd ever seen in my life.

"I know what this is about," she said with that same Latin accent she had the last time we'd messed around.

But there was no way I was letting it happen again. Not like that.

"Put your clothes back on, Lauren," I told her as she moved in even closer to me.

She snatched my shirt open and started kissing my chest. Then I just grabbed her arms and stopped her from doing anything else. I hated seeing her that way.

"You need help, Lauren," I said.

She laughed again.

"What did she tell you?" she asked.

"What did *who* tell me?" I replied."

"Gina!" she demanded. "I'm not stupid. The two of you… conspiring against me. Well, I'm not as crazy as you think!"

"I don't know what you're talking about, baby," I said. "And I didn't say you were crazy. I said you needed help."

"What the fuck is a goddamn counselor going to do for me, Greg?! Huh?!" she asked as she rolled her head back and just kept laughing and laughing. "Fix me? Is that what you think? I don't need fixing, Greg!"

I took a deep breath and tried to keep myself together as Gregory screamed in the distance. It broke my heart to see the only woman I've ever loved going through some shit I couldn't help her out of. We had been through so much together and we always figured life out, whatever it threw at us. But this… what the fuck was this?!

"I just think that all of this shit is fucking with your head, baby," I told her as tears rolled down my face. "I just want you back."

* * *

Vintage chairs, dim lights and poorly selected floral wallpaper surrounded me. Plaques of honor, random figurines and a wall-to-wall bookcase introduced me to a woman who was accomplished, ageless and addicted to psychological thrillers - much like myself. After a few moments of waiting on her brown, leather sofa —the only decent piece of furniture in the room— she smiled as she closed and locked the door to her office and took a seat across from me.

"Thank you for coming in to see me, Lauren," she said, almost as if I was there to visit an ill friend in the hospital.

"Thank you, Dr. Lewis," I replied.

At first, I took the lead, responding to all of her questions and filling her in on the delicate details of my childhood, college life and career, and cultivating conversations that I thought she might enjoy. I had entered her office feeling quite sure of myself. I was only really there because the two people closest to me thought that it was a good idea to see someone, so my plan was to satisfy their requests, return home and continue to allow the misery of motherhood to drown me… at least until I could gain some type of control over my emotions again. Besides, I didn't see a single picture of any children in the woman's office, so I was one hundred percent sure that, even if I did share certain things with her, she wouldn't understand anyway. And there was no way in hell that I was going to risk her judgment!

But after a while, I found it incredibly difficult to maintain eye contact with her.

"Lauren?" she asked as my head hung low, "do you want to tell me what you're feeling right now?"

I definitely felt *something*, but I couldn't find the words to tell her so I just sat there, my fingers fidgeting, my tears dripping down onto my clutch.

"Lauren, are you still in there?" she asked after a stream of silence.

And as I felt every hair rise up across the back of my neck, the blood traveling through every vein in my body, I knew that I wasn't and that a catastrophe beyond my control was on the horizon.

13

The Catastrophe

I think that at one point or another, all of us —Kenneth and I, Evelyn, Gina and even Nathan and a few others— volunteered to babysit little Gregory while Lauren attended her weekly counseling sessions with Dr. Lewis. Gregory had even offered to make adjustments to his work schedule to accommodate Lauren but she insisted on taking the baby along with her.

"He's just not ready to be apart from me, mom," she would tell me every time I reminded her that I was available to look after him.

I didn't want to pressure her because I knew that she was having such a difficult time already. So, after a while, I just left it alone and trusted that she knew what was best for him. He was *her* child, after all, and I didn't want to step on her toes because I knew that feeling all too well.

My mother hated every single thing about the way Kenneth and I were raising Lauren. She hated that I chose not to alter Lauren's natural hair texture because she thought that she looked disorderly and that a proper girl needed to have straight hair. I strongly disagreed. She hated that I allowed Lauren to select her own school clothes because she didn't like the idea of girls wearing clothing that made them look too grown up. She hated the thought of Kenneth changing Lauren's diapers or helping her get dressed because her personal experiences had resulted in her distrust of men. And she hated the fact that we allowed Lauren to have her own voice because she believed that children had a place and Kenneth and I believed that children's voices were just as valid as ours were. So, although my mother and I were quite close, she and I bickered quite frequently, at least where parenting was concerned, and I vowed to myself that Lauren and I would never have to deal with that sort of thing.

I would often wonder, however, if my decision was the best choice. Perhaps I could have offered to sit with little Gregory in the lobby of the counselor's office or maybe even waited in the car, I suppose. None of that happened so I will never know what might have been but I do wonder and I'm not very satisfied with what I consider to be the consequences of my actions - or lack thereof.

So, Kenneth and I had gone over to Lauren and Gregory's home for a visit one afternoon. She had declined my telephone requests to visit on multiple occasions and I had, quite frankly, gotten pretty tired of hearing her opposition, so we just did as Kenneth suggested. We arrived unannounced. You should have seen the look on Lauren's face! She was absolutely stunned!

"What are you guys doing here?" she asked as we walked through the front door and right past her like we owned the place.

"Hello, dear," I replied. "Your father and I were shopping nearby and thought we'd surprise you," I told her.

Now, that wasn't entirely truthful but I considered it to be a small white lie. I just wanted to see my daughter and my grandson. And I wasn't willing to hear "no" from her again. Kenneth went outside and started working around the house with Gregory while Lauren and I sat inside and caught up with one another. But her energy was completely off and I could feel in my heart that something was wrong.

She seemed a bit agitated but she had mentioned that little Gregory had been fussy all night so I just assumed that she was tired, as I imagined any mother would be. I had inquired about the status of the investigation, you know, the incident with Gregory's car. I felt terrible for them. It was just so unfortunate! Not only were Lauren's early days of motherhood clearly taking a toll on her, she and Gregory were dealing with matters of safety in and around their own home. It just wasn't fair.

"The police don't care, mom," she said.

And as far as I could tell, she was right. A great deal of time had passed and apparently, the investigation was at a standstill. Not a single suspect had been brought in for questioning and I found that to be especially odd. As we sat and talked, I noticed that Lauren had become quite distracted by something, although I wasn't sure what it was at the time.

"What's the matter, sweetheart?" I asked as she squinted her eyes and anxiously scanned the room like she was hoping to swat a fly on the loose.

But she didn't say anything. She pressed her index finger into her lips as she stood to her feet, remained silent and started walking toward the kitchen. I thought that was very peculiar but I just sat there holding little Gregory while he slept, not really sure what else to do. I had grown suspicious that Lauren was going through a bit more than she had previously shared with me but I certainly was not expecting what ultimately came to be.

* * *

Lauren wasn't too keen on having strangers over at the house during that time, so when she and Gregory decided they were going to install some new lights around the outside of the house, he figured it was best to just do it himself. He told me that she had been paranoid and although I appreciated what he was doing to ease her mind, I was worried. Sure, she had been having a tough time adjusting to motherhood, but paranoid? That didn't sound like my baby girl.

"You sure you got it?" I asked Gregory as I looked up at him on that ladder over the garage.

"Yeah, I'm good," he said.

Now, this might be a little off-topic but I did think it was strange that so many stray cats kept walking up in the driveway toward the house. I just stomped them away because I knew how my daughter felt about them. She always hated them, ever since she was a little girl. And I've never too much cared for them, myself. I'm more of a dog man. Dogs are loyal and all they want is for you to love them. Cats, on the other hand, are mysterious… a little too mysterious for my liking. They're strange, really.

So anyway, I stood out there, passing tools and light bulbs to Gregory as he needed them… just two grown men talking. I enjoyed spending time with Gregory, you know, any chance I got and although it had been quite a while and the circumstances weren't the best, it was good to be there with him.

"So, how long you planning on renting these cars?" I asked him.

"Just until I find something I really want," he said.

It really didn't make no damn sense to me why somebody would just go into another man's driveway, tear up their car and go on about their business. I mean, they didn't even try to steal nothing. And surely there was something they could've taken. Loose change from the cup holder, tools out the trunk... maybe even the battery from under the hood. Something.

You know, years ago, when I was a young fellow, my Buick quit on me while I was taking the freeway out to a job interview. So, I called my buddy, JP, and had him pick me up and drive me to the interview. Now, my plan was to go borrow enough money from my Pops to have my car towed to a shop first thing the next morning. Boy, I got back out to that freeway that next morning where I had left my car, and somebody had busted my windows out, got under my hood and took my battery right on out the car. I was so mad! I didn't get the job either and there I was with no car, no money, no job and no way to find out who had taken my battery. It was a mess! But anyhow... back to the story.

So, I asked Gregory, "Did the police find the punks who did it?"

He told me they hadn't and I just couldn't quite understand that. Too much time had passed, surely they should have figured out something by then. You know, I could tell that Gregory had a lot on his mind and I didn't blame him. There he was trying to keep his family safe from something that he couldn't explain while Lauren was going through some mess that she probably couldn't explain either.

"How's Lauren holding up?" I asked him.

He told me, "She's having a hard time. When she's not paranoid, she's going off on me about something. And just when I think we're good, she flips the script. Lauren is… different," he said. "Sometimes, I don't really know *who* I'm dealing with."

It really pained me to hear those things about Lauren, you know. And although it didn't sound like the Lauren I knew, I wasn't surprised. I had been over to visit her and the baby one day while Gregory was at work and I noticed something different about her, myself. But what I saw wasn't nothing I hadn't already seen in my lifetime before. She seemed a little on edge - watching and listening for that monitor while the baby slept. And just the way she kept on looking out the window and reacting to little sounds around the house. You know, house sounds. So I asked her how she was feeling. We always been real close, Lauren and I, so I thought she would open up to me, you know?

"I'm fine, Daddy," she said, even though the sadness in her eyes told me that she wasn't.

"Come on, sit down next to me," I told her. "Take a load off."

She was hesitant at first but she finally sat down on the couch next to me.

"You know, when you were a baby," I said, "you just cried and cried and cried and it seemed like the only person in the world who could calm you down was me. Seemed like as soon as I walked into the room, the crying would stop. Almost like… like you could feel my presence," I told her.

The more I talked, the more tears just started running down her face.

"Now, your mother," I continued, "she didn't handle that too well at first. She thought you didn't like her."

You see, her mother hit a rough patch after Lauren was born and I wanted her to know that because I thought it might make her feel a little better about her own situation. It took Robin a while but she made it through and I was sure that Lauren would, too. She asked me if I thought she was crazy.

"Hell, Lauren we're all a little crazy," I told her. "But baby, being a parent is hard work and when you got other things going on around you, that don't make it no easier."

I could tell that what I said had struck a nerve with her because the tears just poured out of her eyes. But then, just all of a sudden, she hopped up off the couch, turned and looked at me and just started giggling like a young girl or something or other. She wiped her eyes and just went to cleaning the house like everything was alright. It was the strangest thing and it gave me the strangest feeling.

* * *

As I sat there talking to my mother, as happy as I was to have her there with me, I found it difficult to really be present with her. I was very distracted by this loud, repetitive thudding sound in the distance. I wasn't sure what it was but I could hear my name being called in the midst of it. So, rather than just sit there and wonder, I decided to go see for myself. And even though I didn't know what it was, I had this feeling that whoever had entered our home before was there again, and this time, I wasn't going to sit by frightened, waiting on Greg or another ridiculous police officer to tell me that I was making it all up.

The sound grew closer and became even more intense the farther I got into the kitchen. It was coming from the basement and there was no longer any doubt in my mind… someone was there! I pulled the largest butcher knife I could find from the block on the counter, opened the basement door and followed the sound down the stairs.

"Who's here?" I inquired as I moved around our large, gray sectional like a predator on the prowl for her prey.

It was then that I noticed a light coming from inside the room down the hallway. I took a deep breath as I cautiously proceeded toward the light. Outside of the door now, I pressed my back against the wall as I slowly pushed the door open and entered the room. I lowered the knife and relaxed against the wall when I realized that the sound was coming from the dryer! I had forgotten that I'd put a load of clean clothes in just before my parents arrived. I must have overloaded it.

Tears rolled down my cheeks as I took another deep breath and attempted to settle my racing heart. Then suddenly, I gasped, clenched the knife and lunged toward the sound of heavy footsteps coming right at me!

* * *

"Lauren?!" I called out as I grabbed the knife and tussled with her as she continued to attack me. "Baby, it's me!" I assured her. "It's just me!"

I don't know if I will ever forget the look she gave me. She looked… like she had seen a ghost or something maybe even worse. I pulled her in close to me, wrapped my arms around her and held her as she sobbed. I could feel her heart pounding, almost like it was my own.

"I'm so fucking tired Greg," she whispered as she surrendered.

That moment still follows me… but sadly, it isn't the only one.

One night, I was giving Gregory a bath. I knew that Lauren had had a long day with him so when I came home from work, I told her to go ahead and get herself cleaned up and I encouraged her to take some time to herself. So, she handed him over to me and I just assumed that she was going to get in the shower. I got the baby washed and dressed, gave him a bottle and read to him until we both fell asleep. When I woke up a couple of hours later and realized that I was still in the nursery, I carefully laid Gregory down in his crib and went on out the room.

I noticed that the lights from the surveillance monitors were on as I started to pass by the office. Even though I would keep the system running through the night, I always turned the monitors off because they gave off a lot of bright light and it was disturbing. So, I took a look in the office and Lauren was in there. Her head was just jerking back and forth between the monitors, like some type of animal. She was fidgeting - her fingers traumatizing the screen as she alternated between the different areas of the house.

"Lauren?" I called out, more concerned than ever before.

She turned around quickly with these… evil-looking eyes and with that deep voice that I had only heard once before.

"Leave me the fuck alone!" she hollered out.

So, I flipped the light switch on to get a better look at her. I walked on into the office and based on the way she looked at me, she didn't like me being there.

"Whoa, whoa, baby. Relax," I said as I gently touched her arm. "You're gonna drive yourself crazy watching these cameras like this. Come on. Give it a rest for tonight, alright?" I told her.

She dropped her head, closed her eyes and just sat there.

"Do you hear that?" she softly asked after several moments of silence.

"Hear what?" I asked as I moved in a little closer to her.

"Those voices, Greg," she said. "They won't stop calling… my name."

I just grabbed her, you know, and held her close to me.

"You're tired, baby," I told her, wanting to believe that *that* was the reason.

But honestly, I was terrified and after we finally went to bed, I couldn't fall asleep because I couldn't stop worrying about her. Gregory's first hunger cry was around one o'clock in the morning and after what had happened, I didn't think she'd be ready to get up and feed him.

"You want me to go?" I asked, knowing that she hadn't had much rest.

Lauren always kept a freezer full of bottles of the milk she'd pumped so I was more than willing to take care of it if she wasn't up to nursing him.

"It's fine," she said as she hopped out of bed, grabbed her robe from the foot of it, slid her feet into her slippers and left the bedroom.

She came back to bed about twenty minutes later and his second cry was just before four. Her arms flopped to her side as she pulled herself up out of bed, grabbed her robe, put her slippers back on and left again. Couple of hours later, same thing. Next cry, she pounded her fists into the mattress and kind of whimpered as she climbed out of bed. I don't even think she knew that I was watching her. I just laid right there all night long, my mind racing as I tried to figure out what my next move should be. But my mind was filled with confusion.

So much confusion.

Was I ever worried that she might try to hurt Gregory? I definitely should have been but I wasn't. I had never seen her do anything to him that made me think about that. The Lauren that I knew wouldn't hurt a soul. The Lauren that I knew bounced back from whatever knocked her down. She was resilient, confident and brave. She was more put together than any other woman I had ever encountered. And the Lauren that I knew was in control of her life and would never allow anyone or anything to get in the way of her being the woman she wanted to be. But this... this wasn't the Lauren I knew.

14

The Confusion

When my buddy, Nate, first told me that his older brother, Greg, and his wife, Lauren, was looking for personal security, I was geeked! First of all, me and Nate… we go way back. So, I trusted him and I already knew it was legit, right? Second, now I didn't tell nobody this at first but my girlfriend at the time, Sharisse… we didn't break up or nothing, we just pre-engaged right now, so yeah. But anyway, Sharisse was a *real* big fan of Lauren's so when I told her about the opportunity she was all on my ass!

"Hell yeah, you betta take that job," she said. "You never know what type of exclusive books we can get for free, so don't be around here acting stupid! Don't play with me!"

So, I thought about what she said. The money was more than I had ever made on any gig *and* they was Black. Not that I needed a whole lot of convincing, but I was all in. But I'm a professional, you feel me? So, I had to play it cool and act like I needed some time to make a decision. I didn't.

At first, the gig was pretty solid. Most of the time, I just stayed close to Lauren, and Greg too, when he wasn't working, just making sure they was good. I even got to do some traveling. First time going to Europe - being around all them fancy ass white people. It was clean as hell over there, too. And expensive! But, I didn't really have to pay for nothin', so I just did my job and acted like I knew which fork to use or what color napkin to ask for. *Shit...* I didn't! But, I wasn't gon' let them know that. You feel me?

You know it's some crazy ass people out there and Lauren was famous as hell, so I had to keep my eyes on her. She could be doing the most basic shit, too, like sniffing all the body washes in Target or returning a dress to the mall, and here come lil' Miss Meagan from Michigan, crying and shit.

Talkin' 'bout, "Oh, my gosh, *it's really you*. Your words really spoke to me, Lauren. I feel seen."

Just stupid. Of course you feel seen, bitch! We see you. But it didn't matter if it was Meagan, Michelle or LaMonte Evans from the South side —you know he go both ways— Lauren loved her fans, and if they asked for that autograph, you better believe she was gon' smile and give it to 'em. Lauren was a sweet lady and I guess you could say that I had a special place in my heart for her, I really did. Tell you the truth, her and my gra'mama had the same name, so I knew she had to be good people and I for damn sure wasn't letting nothing happen to her... not on my watch. Hell no!

But yeah, everything was copesthetic up until Lauren had that baby, Lil' Greg. He was cute, too. Now, I won't say that her career ended but it definitely hit a standstill. I went from escorting her into her car from this event she had done up in Toronto to finding out that her water had broke and her next however many events had been canceled. It was so abrupt and I just assumed I was out of a job. That was until Greg hit me up some months after the baby was born asking if I would be willing to come out and secure they house while he worked.

"This house is nice as hell, man," I told him when I first stepped foot inside.

I'm talking 'bout shit you see in a movie. Man, I hadn't never seen no real life spiral staircase or no… no big old couch like that. Nice! You feel me? Marble on the flo'! They shit was nice! So anyway, Greg thanked me for coming after so much time had passed and I was just happy to be back in the game. I had been looking for work for a while, so the timing was perfect.

Greg was a little vague, though, when I asked him what the deal was because, based on what I was seeing, shit just didn't add up. He started talking about somebody broke in and somebody fucked his car up. I used to love that car, too, especially them creamy peanut butter seats! They wasn't no normal peanut butter seats, neither. They was exclusive. That shit was slick!

So, then Greg told me that Lauren was a little different from the last time I had seen her, but even if he hadn't said nothing, it wouldn't have been that hard for me to pick up on it on my own. Me and Greg was talking for a minute then Lauren came down the stairs with the little baby in her arms, his lil' fat self. Small, but damn, looked just like his daddy. It was wild! Same ear shape, same dimples and everything! But Lauren looked a mess when I saw her. Her eyes was all sunk in… you know that 'possum look people be getting when they on that stuff? Yeah, you know what I'm talkin' 'bout. She spoke to me but not like *spoke*-spoke.

She used to holla at me like, "hey, what's up, Malcolm. How are you?" with a lil' smile.

But, that day, she was more like, "somebody take this damn

baby… oh hi." So, it was different.

She didn't do it exactly like that but she might as well had, you know what I'm sayin'? So, I started watching the house and at first, it was cool - a big change from following her around town or traveling to different countries like before. The neighborhood was pretty much quiet during the day when Greg was gone to work. Only person I ever really saw was they neighbor, Mrs. Banfield… this old ass, nosey-ass white lady that wouldn't let me out of her sight. Every time I looked anywhere around that mothafucka, I'm locking eyes with Mrs. Banfield and all them damn cats. I don't even know if the cats was hers or if they was strays because she was holding them and they was purring while she was rubbing them and shit, but then it was like they was on they own because I kept seeing them sitting on top of other people's mailboxes, in they front yards, walking down the street… they even tried to get up in Greg and Lauren's house, sniffing all them purple flowers and shit. But I clapped the hell out of they asses until they took off. Cats ain't like dogs. You clap or buck at a dog and he out. You do that same shit to a cat… they ass ain't moving.

They just look at you like, "nigga what?" like they ain't scared of nothing!

But day in and day out, Lauren just sat up in that house. Sometimes she spoke to me, sometimes she looked out the window at me like she didn't even know who I was.

"You alright in there, Ms. Lauren?" I always asked because like I said… not on my watch!

And whether or not she answered me, sooner or later I would catch her moving around inside the house, so I knew she was good. I would stay out there for most of the day, circling the property, making sure nothing foul was going on, and every time Greg pulled back into the driveway, I felt good because I knew I had done my job.

And every day, Greg would just be like, "See you tomorrow," so I knew I was back like I never left.

The pay was even better than before, too. The location was nice and quiet and I could talk to Sharisse whenever I felt like it because I was just out there by myself… and Mrs. Banfield old sneaky ass. But for the most part, it was real good… until it wasn't, you feel me?

So, this is how the craziest shit that I have ever been a part of —and I have been a part of some crazy shit— all went down! It was a Thurs'dy. Greg took off to work, as usual. He hugged and kissed Lauren and the baby, we gave each other some dap and he pretty much just got in the car and left.

Now, let me just say this… Me and Sharisse was up real late the night before because she wanted to watch some wack-ass movie that was supposed to be scary but it wasn't, so I was sleepy as hell. I wasn't sleeping on the job but I was *dozing* on the job. It ain't the same but I still kept my shades on because I didn't want nobody to see my eyes rolling back in my head, just for them to run back and tell Greg and for me to lose my job. No, thank you. And when I say *nobody*, I'm talkin' 'bout Banfield. Y'all already know.

Anyway, it was just like any other day at first. And like I said before, the house was big, so I didn't usually hear much from Lauren anyway unless she had something to say to me, which she rarely did. That day, I did hear the baby crying for a while but then I heard Lauren singing to him and after about ten minutes, that was pretty much it. I didn't hear nothing else. Sidebar though, Lauren did have a nice lil' voice on her but I swear on my gra'mama grave, I ain't never heard no nursery rhyme like that before. That shit was creepy as fuck and I was glad when she stopped singing it. Had chills runnin' up and down my spine. And what I look like being scary? I'm supposed to be the safe one.

Moving on though, I just kept doing my job, you know, how I had been doing. And when Greg came in from work, we both said "what's up," slapped hands, then all that peaceful shit went out the window in just a matter of seconds. I'm sure y'all heard about some crazy shit but y'all ain't gon' even be able to believe me when I tell y'all what happened next.

* * *

Lauren had become almost obsessed with this idea that somebody was out to destroy our family but my biggest concern was her. I needed to be at work but I also needed some type of assurance that she and Gregory were good while I was away. My mama, her parents, Gina, and even our neighbor, Mrs. Banfield, offered to come over and sit with her during the day but Lauren wasn't having it. So, I had to figure something out. I felt comfortable with Malcolm, he had experience with Lauren and I knew that he was the guy for the job so, I called him up and he was available, so that was that.

Things were going pretty good at first… at least they were while I was at work. I would call and check on Lauren and the baby throughout the day and she seemed fine, whether I talked directly to her or straight to Malcolm. Everything was cool. Shit was still a little tense when I would come home though. Lauren was really going through something and as hard as it was to watch and kinda go through it with her, I felt better knowing that she was at least in counseling or therapy, or whatever she called it, trying to work the shit out.

Lauren had even told me that the therapist —she called her Dr. Lewis— had agreed to doing home visits so that she and the baby wouldn't have to worry about going into her office. I thought it was perfect. I also thought that her behavior was somehow related to her therapy, like… like she was just getting everything out and that even though she seemed to be getting worse, maybe it was just a part of the process. You know, like when you're starting a new product for your skin and sometimes your face starts purging. It might last a while but once all of the bad shit is out, you're good. So, I just kinda looked at it that way, like Lauren was purging. She even told me that Dr. Lewis had prescribed her something to make her feel better.

"You're not crazy, baby," I told her as tears rolled down her face just before she took the first pill.

This was huge because as long as I had known Lauren, she refused to take *any* medicine. She didn't take Tylenol or Ibuprofen. It's the reason she opted out of the epidural when she had Gregory. She just didn't want to put something inside of her body that might end up doing more harm than good, so she always tried to find a natural way to treat whatever the issue was. But I don't think she had the mental strength at that time to figure out another plan, so she thought it was best to just take the medicine. And I supported her.

It was rough at first but after a few weeks, I started noticing a change. Lauren was happy again. I could tell that she was really bonding with the baby. We had started back making love. Even our family noticed the change in her and everybody was glad to see the old Lauren again. She and I even decided to throw a little house party, you know, just to see everybody and really just to welcome our Lauren back.

It was fun. Real fun. Upbeat music was playing, family and friends was mixing, mingling and munching on snacks. I was playing cards with the fellas at the round table and Lauren was gossiping with the girls on the sofa. It felt like old times, to be honest. But Lauren, or whoever the hell she had become at that point, really had us fooled.

Ms. Robin was upstairs with the baby when shit really started to shift.

"Lauren, sweetheart will you grab me a bottle?" she called down. "This child is hungry, again," she said.

I was about to just get the bottle myself but Lauren eagerly hopped up off the sofa and walked into the kitchen. My mom was already in there doing something, so she was the one that brought the shit to *my* attention. She told me that Lauren came in, opened the refrigerator door, and grabbed the bottle but when she closed the door, she paused and narrowed her eyes and just kinda stood there with her eyes twitching.

"It's just odd, that's all I'm saying. I've never seen anything like it, myself," she told me.

I told her what I believed, you know. That we were good and that Lauren was doing so much better than before. And even though she smiled and said alright, I could tell that she didn't believe any of it. But as the party went on, Lauren started acting really, really strange. She went from my warm and cheerful Lauren to loud and tipsy, and as long as I've known her, she had never acted that way.

"Ohhhh, Mamacita's back! OoohLaLa!" I heard her say as she started dancing around and running her hands through my mama's hair.

My mama did not like that shit and I could tell that everybody else was kinda uncomfortable, too. I tried to get her to sit down and chill out, drink some water or eat something to calm herself down but she just kept getting louder and more aggressive. The shit was embarrassing, but I wasn't gonna just abandon her. Everybody was watching her and watching me, too, trying to figure out what I was gonna do, I guess. It didn't go on too much longer because her dad wasn't having it.

"It's time to go," he said as he stood up and shut the whole party down.

Everybody left and that was pretty much it. I took Lauren upstairs, cleaned her up, got her to bed, and besides the baby waking up a few times to eat, she slept it off. The next morning, she slept in a little bit, so I fed Gregory, made us something to eat and went on to work. Malcolm was at the house so I felt pretty good about it. But on my ride in to work, I started thinking: Lauren wasn't a drinker like that. She was breastfeeding and there was no way she was gonna let alcohol get to her milk. How could she have been tipsy, you know what I mean? So, I was a little bit worried about her, I can't lie. Something wasn't right. And there was no way in hell that anybody could have prepared us for what happened when I got home from work that evening and walked inside the house.

It was dark inside and there was this sick, disgusting odor that I can almost smell now. Like something... raw but sweet or... I don't know man. It was bad. Just know that. So, I put my briefcase down on the floor and just covered my nose.

"Lauren?" I called out.

But she didn't say a word. And when I turned the light on, my heart just started shaking. Man, it looked like a damn slaughterhouse in there! There was blood, hair, garbage... everywhere! I took off through the house, calling out Lauren's name! I just knew that she and the baby was dead. I knew it! As I went through the house, I kept seeing all this blood and shit and I kept wondering why I had been so trusting of Lauren with the baby. Man, I had all types of shit going on in my head. But as I was almost up the stairs, I heard this Earth-shattering scream. It was Gregory! My heart just dropped.

* * *

Dog, I was headed to my car and I wasn't gon' turn back around but all that damn screaming… *shit*, I wasn't about to go to jail for nobody and y'all for damn sure wasn't gon' see my lil' ass on one of them true crime documentaries. No siree! My hands was shakin' and shit but I was finally able to get my phone out my pocket so I could call the police. I was nervous as hell!

But I just told them, "Something is going down up over here! Everybody screaming and shit… Hell, I don't know what's going on but y'all need to get somebody out here, and quick too!"

I had only brought a couple of bullets with me 'cause that shit's expensive and I didn't even really know how to use that mothafucka! Oops, excuse my French. I've been cussing a lot, huh? Man, don't you judge me. I'm working on myself, alright? Going to church and shit, trying to get right. You should've seen the suit I had on last Sunday. Sharisse picked it out. Pinstriped… navy blue with the gold trim. That shit was fire! I don't even know why I just said "fire". My nephew be talking like that, you know he young and shit so that's his generation, not mine. It's a lil' confusing to me, right? Cause fire is supposed to be bad, ain't it? That shit will burn your ass up, have you walking around here with two or three different skin tones or a mushed up nose. So, I be confused but that's his choice, not mine. You must don't cuss, do you?

So anyway, I hung up the phone, examined my pistol —which I almost dropped, by the way— took me a deep breath and turned back around to the house. I knew what I had to do. I busted through that door like I was a bad boy or somebody! Well, I didn't really *bust*-bust through it because that shit was heavy, but goddamn! My eyes immediately bulged, I gagged and almost threw the fuck up! I don't do blood! I do not do blood. So, back out the house my ass went!

And Mrs. Banfield old ugly ass looked at me talking about, "Is everything alright in there?"

"Naw, bitch!" I told her. "It ain't! Do it sound alright?" Nosey ass!

15

The Choice

Gregory's scream was nearby but I wasn't sure where he was just yet. He wasn't in the nursery and I had checked pretty much everywhere else in the house so I went down the hall to our bedroom, because I thought that maybe both of them were in there. Streaks of bright, red blood nearly covered the room. Blood dripped from Lauren's face as she rocked back and forth at the edge of the bed, holding Gregory in one arm. Her torn clothes hung from her body and her hair was bathing in the blood as she gazed into the distance, fidgeting her fingers against this warn leather bible that she kept packed away in her closet. She was humming what sounded like "Hush Little Baby", but the whole thing had me shook. Thought my heart was about to explode.

"Lauren, what the hell happened?!" I cried out as I grabbed my screaming baby and wrapped my arms around Lauren.

But she just glared through the open door and down the hallway while I tried to check her out. I couldn't see where the blood was coming from and Gregory only had a little on him. But if there was that much blood, how could Lauren still be alive, you know? But then she started laughing and I knew that this shit was so much worse than I imagined.

I pushed back and stood to my feet and was just like, "Baby?"

But Lauren suddenly stiffened her face and without even looking at me she said, "That bitch tried to kill me."

"Who?" I asked as I started looking around the room.

But she just kept on repeating herself and I couldn't get nothing else out of her. I took Gregory and we quickly left out the room because I wanted to lay eyes on that surveillance tape. It had to have some answers. I just kept wondering how Malcolm had missed all of that.

Man, that shit was pure gore! Like something out of a scary movie. And I couldn't understand how he hadn't heard anything. So, I rewound the footage and I just sat there in shock, tears just falling out of my eyes as the whole thing unfolded right in front of me.

One of the clips showed Lauren leaving out the front door and at the same, Malcolm was pacing the backyard. She walked up to this flock of cats in the driveway and started feeding and playing with them and pretty much just lured them into the house with this large pot of food.

Now, I don't know if you remember me saying this but, Lauren always hated cats. Never in a million years would she be playing with them, let alone bringing them in our house.

So, in another clip, I saw them damn cats spreading all around over the family room, and out of nowhere, Lauren took this big ass butcher knife and started slaughtering 'em. Blood was flying in every direction, and she didn't stop until she got 'em all - grabbing and chasing 'em like a maniac. It was insane!

I couldn't see him on the tape at first but I could hear Gregory crying. The whole time all of this shit was happening, Lauren was singing "Hush Little Baby". It looked like she was getting rid of all of her emotions right there in that room as she sliced the life out of them cats. It was brutal and I never knew she could be capable of doing anything like that. It was hard. It was real hard to sit and watch it all. But if these cats had been killed in my house, where were they now? That's what *I* wanted to know.

* * *

The police was taking way too long to get there so I called they asses back.

"Where the fuck are you guys at?" I asked 'em in my white voice. "I just went up in there and there is blood all over that motherfucker!"

Now, I normally just say "mothafucka," you know, like with the "uh" sound in the middle and at the end… Ebonics, right? But I was trying to be professional because I was in my uniform and I thought that maybe if they thought I was white, it would make 'em move faster. Because y'all already know, if this was a white family, they would've been there before we got off the phone the first time. But no, they wanted to discriminate. And I wasn't having that shit.

* * *

I just remember hearing what sounded like a gun click behind me. I cautiously turned around in the chair, not knowing what to expect, and there Lauren stood in the doorway.

"Lauren? Baby, why did you do this?" I asked her, hoping to

make sense of what was happening.

But she just giggled, pressed the gun into her lips and moved in closer to me.

"Shh," she said as she pushed her lips out, "I won't let them hurt you. I promise."

"Give me the gun," I told her. "You don't have to do this."

My heart was breaking, seeing her like that. But then she said something that… that just made me feel like… like this woman that I had planned to spend the rest of my life with… like she was just gone and… and… I felt. I'm sorry.

She looked at me and said, "None of the others have ever loved you the way that I love you, and now, none of them ever will."

I knew then that this shit was bigger than the both of us. I ain't never been no punk, but I felt like a scared little boy as she laughed, mocked me and bullied me with that gun. I don't even know where the fuck the gun came from, to be honest with you.

"Lauren, baby just talk to me. What *is* this?" I asked as I held Gregory a little bit tighter, still hoping for answers.

But as I stood to my feet, that gun guiding me out of that office, I started to believe that there were no answers.

"It's just you and me now, forever," she said as she smiled and nudged me down the hallway.

She closed her eyes and twisted her lips as Gregory's scream returned and quickly intensified. Then she waved the gun in the air and just lost it.

"Shut the fuck up!!" she yelled out.

I tried to talk to her. I tried to remind her that he was just a baby… *her* baby. I told her that she was scaring him, and I remember how confused she looked when I said that.

"I am protecting him, Gregory!" she yelled out.

She hadn't called me Gregory since the day we met, when she asked if I minded if she called me Greg instead. I didn't mind.

"Do you have any idea what they would do to you if they got in this house?" she carried on.

I didn't. And I had no idea who she was talking about.

"You stopped taking your pills?" I asked as we approached the top of the stairs.

"What pills?" she replied as she laughed me off.

I felt like such a coward as she pointed that gun at my baby and made me take him down into the basement. But what was I gonna do, huh? That wasn't Lauren. That was... some monster. I didn't know who she was... but at the same time, I knew exactly who she was. She was... my wife. I didn't want to hurt her. I didn't want her to hurt herself or the baby. Or me. But whose side was I on, you know? In that moment, whose side was I on?!

So, the three of us were down in the basement. I was holding Gregory on the couch, bouncing him, just trying to keep him calm. And Lauren was just circling us, reciting this scripture that I hadn't heard since I was little boy.

"Who can find a virtuous woman?" she began. "For her price is far above rubies. The heart of her husband doth safely trust in her, so that he shall have no need of spoil. She will do him good and not evil all the days of her life," she went on.

That bible was a wedding gift from her mom's friend, Ms. Carol. It had sat in Lauren's closet in the same package that it came in. Lauren was spiritual but she didn't believe most of what was in the bible. So, it really blew my mind that she knew this scripture so well. Maybe she remembered it from *her* childhood, too. I don't know.

"Lauren, maybe we should give Dr. Lewis a quick call," I suggested, hoping to reason with her. "I'm sure she'll be more than happy to talk us through this."

I hadn't spoken with Dr. Lewis before but I figured I could at least try.

"Forsake her not, and she shall preserve thee: love her, and she shall keep thee," Lauren continued.

And then, she suddenly stopped, tilted her head to one side and slowly approached me and the baby. I was boiling inside as she started stroking Gregory's little face with her pistol. I didn't want to just sit there and let the shit happen but I also didn't want to do anything that would cause her to slip up and shoot one of us. I didn't know what to do. Then, she started back up with that song, "Hush Little Baby". She grinned, like she was happy and satisfied with herself then pulled the pistol up to *my* face.

"Gregory and Alicia sitting in a tree…" she started singing in this crazy, playful way. "K-I-S-S-I-N-G. First comes love—."

"Alicia?" I uttered as she continued to stroke my face.

"If they think they're going to get their hands on you," she said, "they've got another thing coming."

I felt lost. But I couldn't just sit there and let this stranger that I loved with all my heart and soul do the unthinkable. So, I took a chance when I decided to play along.

"Alicia?" I called as I wiped my eyes and smiled back at her.

"Yes, honey?" she replied.

"Come here," I insisted. "Why don't you sit down and relax, huh? You've been on your feet for a while and you're probably tired. I'll go upstairs and make you a nice hot cup of tea. Would you like that?" I asked.

She nodded and giggled at the idea as she took a seat right next to me. But when I suggested she hand me the gun, she wasn't having it. She narrowed her eyes, pressed her lips together and just as I tried to slide the gun from her hand, she raised it and backhanded me across the face.

"You think I'm stupid?" she asked. "I'm on your side, Gregory! Why would you try to trick me? Huh?"

She wasn't Lauren but she was just as smart as her.

"Please, just give me the gun," I begged her as I wiped blood from the corner of my mouth. "You don't know what you're doing."

She stood up, her eyes filled with tears, and started slowly backing away from me.

"I warned you!" she roared.

I laid Gregory down on the carpet. I didn't know what else to do with him. And as I started walking toward Lauren she kept backing away from me.

"Give me the gun, baby," I said.

It was then that I think I noticed the trail of blood leading down into the laundry room. And the thump in the distance told me exactly where those dead cats were. That shit was sick and heavy on my heart but I couldn't stop trying to save us all. I get sick to my stomach every time I think about it.

"Take another step and I'll blow your motherfucking brains out!" she exclaimed, but it was too late.

I had just finished taking another step.

"Lauren, please!!!" I cried out as she fired the pistol.

And all I heard was glass shattering behind me and my baby screaming as I ducked. And when I looked up, Lauren was gone. I rushed over to check on Gregory and fortunately, hadn't been shot and neither had I. My heart was racing as I scanned the basement for Lauren. Then I heard a scream in the distance that was so powerful that I felt like the house was being torn apart.

I had a choice to make. I didn't wanna leave my baby behind but I needed to put an end to this shit. And I didn't wanna risk his life any more than I already had. So, I left him on the floor, and I went back upstairs. As I made my way into the kitchen, I could hear this creepy-ass song coming from upstairs. It sounded like it was in Spanish or something and as I started to follow it, I looked down and noticed a trail of lavender lily petals on the floor.

"Lauren?" I cautiously called out as I followed the flowers.

The song got louder as I got closer to our bedroom and it finally stopped when I entered our bathroom.

"Welcome home, Papi. I knew you'd show up sooner or later," Lauren said as she grinned and greeted me with a familiar Latin accent from the center of the steamy bathtub. "I'm talking about you, silly," she said as I looked back. "I can smell your sexy cologne from a mile away."

I called her name again but I knew it wasn't my Lauren and I knew that it wasn't Alicia. She rose up, stepped out of the bathtub and spit at my face as she passed me, water trickling down from her naked body.

"But I guess it's true what they say," she said. "All men really *are* stupid."

I watched as she sashayed over to the bed, grabbed her robe and started fingering the fabric.

"Privileged bitch!" she belted out.

I felt for my phone, but I couldn't find it so I just started backing away from her.

"Oh, you're not going anywhere, Papi," she said as she quickly turned around, placed the pistol against her back and grinned as she followed me. "Those filthy bitches want you and they want you bad, but not as badly as I do."

I nearly pissed my pants, man. I begged her to let me help her. I begged her to give me that gun but she wasn't listening. Her laugh was crazy… psychotic, even.

"You want to help me? Aww, how thoughtful of you," she said. "But riddle me this, Papi…were you thinking of helping me when you were fucking her in *our* bed? Were you thinking of helping me when she was pushing what should have been our babies out of her perfect little body? Hmm?"

I just kept thinking that if there really was a God, I needed his ass right then in order to make it through that shit. As we approached the top of the stairs, Lauren stopped and tilted her head like she was in deep thought.

"I never understood what you saw in her," she said.

I caught my breath *and* myself as I nearly fell backward down the stairs.

"Don't be afraid," she said as I carefully stepped down. "I forgive you because we were meant to be together, and now, nothing is going to stand in the way of that. Believe me. Until death do us part."

My eyes widened as she pulled the gun from behind her back and pointed it right between my eyes. I begged her and I begged her.

"Baby, please!" I cried. "Please, stop".

"Baby?" she asked. "Sounds like *you're* the real baby, doesn't it? My name is Carmen, you asshole!" she boasted as she cocked the gun and fired the pistol once again.

And just like before, I had dodged the bullet and Lauren was on the loose. I looked over and saw that my phone was on the kitchen counter. So, I ran over to it and dialed 9-1-1.

"What's your emergency?" the dispatcher asked at the sound of yet another pistol cock.

As I slowly lowered the phone from my ear, I stood in shock as I faced a very masculine version of my wife. An illuminated cigar hung casually from her lips. After a few moments of dead silence, she took a long, deep draw then removed it from her mouth.

"Who the fuck you think you callin'?" she asked. "Old lame ass. I don't know why these messy bitches out here fightin' over you, punk ass. I should just blow all of y'all's brains out!"

"Who are you?" I mumbled, completely shook by that point.

"Shiddd… Mothafucka," she said as she playfully punched me in the chest, "I'm Larry. And go shut that loud ass baby up before I do it."

I'm kinda embarrassed to say this, but I listened. What choice did I have, you know?

"What do you want?" I asked as I sat there, once again, holding my baby in my arms.

She sat down next to me, relaxed her arm on the back of the sofa and chuckled as she blew smoke into the air.

"Bruh, I want it all," she said as she looked around the room. "This house, yo lady… Shit, I wanted your car but I realized I'd look better in a blue one so I just smashed that shit. It's all good though. I'm forgiven, you feel me? That's what your lady taught me. Forgiveness."

It took everything I had in me not to knock whoever the fuck it was out. It looked like Lauren but it behaved like a linebacker.

"So it was you?" I asked. "You did that to my car?"

This… this person starting laughing, like it was a joke and

after a few seconds, she just stopped and stood up.

"That shit ain't funny!" she said. "Ain't no woman ever made me feel the way yo' lady make me feel and for some reason, all she want is yo lame ass!"

As I sat there holding on to my baby —the only part of Lauren that I felt like I had left— I could hear sirens in the near distance. I couldn't believe what was happening. I just couldn't believe it. It was surreal.

"Should've blown your brains out weeks ago but I let that bitch convince me not to. Now, it's over for yo' ass!" she said as she dropped the cigar on the floor, smashed it with her foot and wiped tears from her face as she carelessly pointed the pistol at me.

"Please don't do this," I cried out for the last time. "Please!"

* * *

Now, I ain't gon' lie: all that blood and shit fucked me up. But I ain't no lil' bitch, so I cracked my knuckles and was getting ready to go back up in there and shut the shit down, you feel me? And just as soon as I grabbed the doorknob, here come the police. Emergency lights filled the street as multiple police cars surrounded the house. Cops filed out of they cars and started moving toward the door. It was just like a movie!!

"What the hell took y'all so long?!" I asked the lil' skinny one in the front. "Everybody up in the house probably dead by now!" I told him.

Man, was I relieved that they showed up though. Sharisse would've killed my ass if I went up in there and died! I can hear her ass now.

Talkin' bout, "Who you think gon' pay for the funeral?"

* * *

"There ain't nothin' I hate more than a beggin' ass mothafucka!" she said as I sat there, crying, at a loss for words.

I could hear that somebody had gotten into the house and Lauren, or Larry or whoever it was, knew it, too.

"You called the cops on me?" she asked.

I hadn't been able to finish my call but I was glad that somebody had stepped in.

"No," I replied, not that it mattered anymore. "It wasn't me."

"You should've just listened," she said and as she pulled the trigger, a police officer's gunfire followed.

I sat there shivering as Lauren closed her eyes, grabbed her head with both hands and screamed as two officers restrained her.

"Sir, is anyone hurt?" this older, female officer asked as she approached me and the baby. And all I could do as I watched these guys take Lauren away was cry. I wasn't ready to let her go, but it felt like I had just witnessed our conclusion.

16

The Conclusion

"'I remember the day as if it were yesterday. I had just finished tidying the office after recovering from an hour-long session with "Jealous Jessie," as I had privately nicknamed him. He was a middle-aged, Mexican-American martial artist from Minnesota who had neglected his thriving career and moved to the Southeast to keep eyes on his newly married ex-wife, who had determined that she'd had enough of his jealous ways. So, it came as no surprise to me that a swiftly acquired restraining order along with a requirement for anger management had landed Jessie a series of psychotherapy sessions with me. I wasn't the most affordable of the therapists in the area, but when reaching the root of an issue was the primary obstacle, *everyone* knew who to call. No, I'm not bragging; however, I am very aware of what I bring to the table and I welcome the casual contester's point of view any day of the week, really.

As I glanced over her file, my mind played with the possibilities for her appointment. We could all benefit from the work of a counselor or therapist at some point in our lives, but "why would a woman of her status require a seat on *my* sofa?"

I wondered just before I opened the door and welcomed her inside.

She was the most fascinating person I had ever encountered, client or otherwise. On the outside, she was *remarkably* stunning. Her chestnut-coated skin elegantly enveloped inside her carefully cultivated couture. Her unapologetic coils placed ever so gracefully around her flawlessly framed face. Her confidence, her poise and her smile. All unmistakably… *perfect.* Her bold brown eyes, however, spoke a complex inner truth that poor Lauren's lips were never quite brave enough to release.

From the moment she first stepped foot inside my office, I knew that both Lauren and I were in for a ride. Where to? I wasn't quite sure. But I trusted my instincts, and the weight of her burdens bullied me further outside my comfort zone than I had ever been before. And it didn't take long for me to realize that I was no longer behind the wheel… if I ever was.

"Lauren Ivory Winters," she proudly announced, in a tone as rasp as it was regal, as I inquired about her intentions.

"You know, my mother always says that real women keep real secrets," she giggled, "but I'll tell *you*, Dr. Lewis… I'm thirty-three. There, I said it."

I smiled and took notes as I listened to what sounded like scripted responses to interview questions that no one had ever even asked. Why on Earth had she really come to see me? And why the fuck did being in her presence make me feel so goddamned… *uneasy?*

Those were the real questions I had. Hell, I already knew her name. I, like most people, was already well aware of what she did for a living, who she was married to and how much their home cost. And a quick Google search provided every other minute detail of her life. Details that, for the purposes of psychotherapy, didn't move the needle one bit. In fact, they were utterly useless pieces of the puzzle that didn't seem to affect the big picture.

In a way, her performance was like being on a date with a beautiful man whose sole intention was to impress me. Sure, that would be pleasant at first, but after a while, I would wish for more than smiles, assurances and stories of his successes. I wouldn't care about his former lovers, how he preferred his eggs cooked or how many children his great Aunt Linda gave birth to during the Great Depression. I imagine I would find those details both premature and less than pertinent to a proper introduction.

In other words, I was rather bored with Lauren and felt forced to sit and absorb an abundance of bullshit when in real life, I would have much rather been getting my car washed and waxed at the new spot on 79th and Lennox. You know, the one with the baby blue archway and the dual entry with the fluorescent peacock decor. Perhaps I'm biased because I absolutely adore birds, but it's tasteful, they were running a grand opening special and it's only two blocks away from my favorite restaurant, Lavender Lily's. I love their couscous stir fry, and I always add on a side of seared Sockeye. Oh, and a small salad! You should try it sometime - if you haven't already.

But rather than allow my personal feelings to jeopardize three decades' worth of prestige and professionalism, I did what any good therapist would do: I listened as she filled my ears with elaborate accounts of her achievements as an accomplished author from Auburn, how she exceeded her parents' expectations and quickly rose to the top of her graduating class at Spelman College an entire year and a half before her advisor's predictions. How she initially committed to being a neurosurgeon but decided against it because math and science weren't quite her thing. And how she had personally designed every little detail of her wedding ceremony decades before she even had a suitor.

But after fifteen pages of notes that seemingly had nothing to do with anything that mattered, I slowly raised my right index finger, just like *my* mother did whenever she needed to excuse herself from the congregation to use the bathroom, spank my bottom or have a bite of the sausage biscuit she kept tucked inside her purse because we were always running late for church. And she would rather snack between songs and scriptures than be titled tardy. Come to think of it - I never did quite understand why my mother raised that finger. Not as a young girl and certainly not now. Who exactly was she seeking approval from? And did she think that by not lifting that finger to excuse herself, the man in the pulpit might make her take her seat? I digress.

"Pardon me, Lauren," I eventually interrupted.

"Yes?" she softly answered.

"Thank you for that information," I said. "I am so sorry to cut you off mid-sentence, but you seemed rather distraught when you called into my office requesting a consultation this morning. But now, you seem quite the opposite. I'm curious. What changed?"

"Oh, that," she said as she chuckled to herself. "No, I am perfectly fine, Dr. Lewis. I guess I just got a little overwhelmed with the baby, and my best friend, Gina, and my husband, Greg, suggested I see someone. That's all. I'm fine, really."

"Hm," I uttered as Lauren's meticulously manicured fingernails fidgeted against her tightly clenched clutch.

"Are you sure, Lauren?" I queried as tears began to puddle over her pupils.

She lowered her head and closed her eyes as thick tears dripped down onto her lap, reminiscent of rain tapping against a rooftop on a gloomy day. And the most spine-chilling seven minutes of my life ensued as a languid Lauren hummed a hair-raising rendition of "Hush Little Baby" while she rocked herself back and forth against the cushions of my couch. Once again, my instincts were right. Lauren was *far* from fine.

"Lauren, are you still in there?" I questioned as I nervously slid to the edge of my chair, knowing good and well that the person sitting across from me was not the same person who had walked into my office.

I had seen file cabinets full of phobias, fears and failed friendships throughout the course of my career, but this… this was something else entirely. And for the first time in my entire adult life, urine trickled down my thighs as the stranger sitting across from me leaned forward, cracked her knuckles and grinned.

"I don't give a damn what none of the others told you about me!" she declared.

As the moisture in my panties grew cold, my heart nearly beat itself out of my chest. I had gone from sheer boredom to a state of bewilderment in the split of a second, and in that moment, I was petrified as this striking young woman *showed* me exactly why my services were necessary. Though I was afraid that I lacked the skills needed to deliver us from this evil, I held on to hope, because although my life felt complete, I was not prepared for my conclusion.

"*Who*, Lauren?" I managed to ask as she reached into her clutch, pulled out a Montecristo Number 4, lit it, took a long steady draw and blew the smoke directly into my nostrils. "Who are the others?"

"You think I don't know, Doctor? You think I don't know how you feel about me?!" she exclaimed as she stood up out of her seat and began to stroll around my office.

My blouse and back became one as sweat rapidly poured from my pores, and my voice, suddenly lost as her raging hands raked across floating shelves, destroying retro replicas, frames filled with fantasies and friends and knickknacks that the Rwandan designer I hired picked up because he felt like they brought a sense of serenity to the space. So much for serenity, Olivier. So much for serenity!

"I've worked my ass to the bone to get where I am!" she roared as she gripped her crotch with one hand and lowered the cigar from her lips with the other, her voice harshened by her heavy inhalations. "No way in hell I'm letting you, a damned kid or the next motherfucker take it all away from me! Fuck that!" she exclaimed.

I cleared my throat as I attempted to take control of the situation.

"Uh, Lauren—" I managed to insert before she shut me up.

"Bitch, I swear to God, you got one more time to call me by her name," she said.

"Well, what… what should I ca-call you then?" I stuttered.

"What the hell else would you call me?" she asked as she chuckled.

"I'm Larry!" she announced as she smashed her cigar straight into the wall.

In that moment, I questioned every single thing that I had ever believed in. I wasn't quite sure how the next seventeen minutes of our session would play out, but there was no doubt in my mind that life was over for me. I knew it was. As mental health professionals, we are taught not to use the term "crazy" when referring to our clients. You know, so they never feel worse than they are already feeling. For empathy's sake. But now, with my life on the line and a stranger in my house, my mind only had the potential to formulate one clear thought: this bitch is crazy!

"Aye, aye, aye," she said as she nearly knocked over the most expensive vase in the room. "Where are my manners?" she innocently asked herself as she turned and trotted toward me, extending one hand to me while fluffing her hair with the other.

I don't know when it happened, but once again, *something* had changed. Her voice. It was… different. The way she pronounced the most common words - the confidence in her tone. And there was now a peculiar accent. Colombian, I think. The way her hips swayed from side to side as she crossed the room with a sense of cool and a spirit of sophistication. The way she scoffed me off when my wimpy handshake didn't satisfy her need for something that I was apparently unequipped to provide.

"What's your problem, honey?" she asked as she turned and returned to her seat. "You sit there with that silly look on your face like I'm not supposed to be here or something. Well, my money is just as good as anybody else's money, alright? I didn't come here for all of this. You don't wanna shake my hand? Then, just say that and I'll leave you alone."

"Lauren?" I questioned.

"Oh," she grunted as she rolled her eyes throughout her head then proceeded to pull a tube of red lipstick from her clutch.

And no, not that modest red that wholesome women wear

when they've reached a certain age that they dare not disclose. This was *red*-red. It was sexy, shameless and enticing.

"That's what this is about," she said. "It's not your fault. I get it - Lauren… Carmen, they're similar. Right? I can't even begin to tell you how many times strangers have approached me on the street, begging for *her* autograph."

I didn't know what to think or how to feel.

"It's comical, really," she laughed.

"But I just sign that bitch's name on their hats or shirts or whatever they want," she admitted. "They don't know the difference. And… and Lauren, she's pathetic! She has no idea how good she has it, and she would rather cry and complain than pick up that pretty face of hers and carry the fuck on. That's what I do when my life gets out of order."

I stared on in both shock and admiration. On the one hand, I was terrified but grateful that Larry had given me a second chance at life. But on the other hand, I was impressed at the seamless switch between Larry and Carmen in just a matter of seconds.

"Carmen?" I asked as she faced herself in a pocket mirror and smoothed the lipstick over her lips. "Do you *know* Lauren?"

"Of course I do," she replied. "Well, I don't *know her*-know her, but I know everything I need to know."

"She mentioned that she'd gotten overwhelmed with her baby," I said, "and that her best friend and her husband suggested she come see me. Do you know anything about that?".

She clapped the mirror shut, stuffed it inside the clutch, crossed her legs and pouted her bright red lips to perfection.

"Listen to me, honey," she said. "A real man would never leave his woman alone to care for a whining baby while he's out running the streets doing who knows what with God knows who. So whatever the hell it is that she's been telling you about her man, don't believe it. Everybody knows that he's a good one, and to tell you the truth, I don't know what he sees in her. That's all I'll say about that."

I took notes, but more than anything else, I was ready to retire.

"Hadn't I helped enough people?" I thought to myself.

I, like Lauren, had graduated early and at the top of my class. I entered this field because I enjoyed guiding people who had lost their way in life and simply needed the motivation to get back on track. But not in this way! In less than one hour, I had witnessed one woman become three, and I knew, without a shadow of a doubt, that all I really had to offer her was a prescription or a referral to the nearest psychiatric facility because being *one* Black woman in America was hard enough as it was. Still is.

But when I lifted my head this time, my heart sank into my stomach. And all of my insecurities soon drifted out the door as the beautiful woman who had come into my office claiming overwhelm sobbed without control. She looked deflated, almost as if she had made it back down to the bottom of a mountain she had never intended to climb.

"Dr. Lewis, the truth is that ever since my son was born," she said, "I haven't felt very much like myself. I'm so lost, and some days I forget where I am or what I've done. Life was good for me, you know?! I had everything a woman could dream of having. The love, family, friends, money and career fulfillment that most people spend their whole lives pretending to have. But it's been months since I've written anything, and when I look in the mirror, sometimes it feels like a stranger is looking back at me. Dr. Lewis, can you help me?" she begged.

Poor Lauren. She *needed* me. It *was* women like her that I had signed up to help! Not Larry or Carmen or whomever the hell else was haunting her. But how the fuck was I, with cold piss sticking to my inner thighs and a wet spot on my back the size of Texas, going to pull that off? I wasn't sure, and I couldn't believe that I was thinking this, but I wanted to give it my best shot.

The hour was up, and I was about to release the *real* Lauren back into the world, because God only knows that there's no more room behind bars for brokenhearted Black mothers or their stray sons who will one day grow up without them. So, that's what I did, and my fear of Lauren and her son's future lingered like Larry's secondhand smoke. No matter where I was or what activities I was engaged in, thoughts of Lauren swallowed me, and my decision to set her free, each time I did, left a lump of uncertainty in my throat.

I became so obsessed with saving Lauren from herself that I began spending every moment of my free time researching outpatient treatment facilities, suspected diagnoses and historical cases of psychosis and mania. My initial assumption was that she suffered from postpartum depression or another related postpartum mood disorder. But her symptoms soon revealed a conglomerate of conditions that I couldn't quite classify as one or the other. And I'm ashamed to admit that I began monitoring her movements or, in other words, stalking her. I could never live with myself if my refusal to admit Lauren backfired and the only way I could control that narrative was to keep a close watch. I terminated all other client relations, and my sole focus became Lauren Ivory Winters.

I suppose I saw pieces of myself in every part of her. Pieces that I had either neglected or had forgotten existed, pieces that I envied and wished for myself. And pieces that felt true to who I was at that moment… a hypocritical hybrid of a human, or so I felt.'"

How was that? I hope I didn't mispronounce or fumble over any words. I'm happy to record it again- if you need me to. You know, I've read that passage more times than I can remember, and still, it brings a wicked chill over my body every time I get to the parts where I effortlessly switch gears. It's unbelievable. But what I find most fascinating is that in those eerie moments, sitting on the sofa in that office —airing out my dirty laundry, if you will— I was not only myself and the assortment of personalities inside of me… *I* was the counselor.

I've been a writer all my life, and even now, I write when my mind finds time for it. And I've created characters with backstories so complex that I often wondered if my readers would be able to follow the narrative. But this was personal. And as grateful as I feel to have been able to tell my story, the Lauren that I was before could have never written such a tale. It's sort of like, as you call it in film, method acting. Only it was method writing, I suppose. Being so deeply rooted in a story that neither you nor those watching can tell the facts from the fiction.

And now, as I sit here with Annie R. - a twenty-seven-year-old whose three-month-old son, Alvin, is living with his grandparents, Peter and Renè, up in Rochester because the voices in Annie's head told her to dangle him over the balcony so that he would stop crying, to my left, and Destiny J. - a forty-two-year-old medical assistant who attempted to kill herself because she ran out of fabric softener sheets, to my right, I would give anything to believe that I don't belong here. But the painful truth is that I do.

* * *

The nights were lonely, the days were heavy, and my life just didn't feel complete without Lauren by my side. I hated waking up in the middle of the night, drenched in sweat because my memories were stuck on repeat, and my mind couldn't tell the difference between the past and the present. Even the strong smell of coffee beans couldn't overpower Lauren's fragrance, a captivating aroma that had become her signature scent over the years. And man, I drunk a *lot* of coffee back then because some nights, I preferred a fight with sleep to the demons roaming around inside my dreams.

But after what felt like forever, I decided to start a new chapter, so I put the house up for sale. I thought it would take a while, but it sold in a couple of weeks. So, Nate and Gina helped me pack up our shit, and me and Gregory moved into an isolated fixer-upper out in the country. I needed the change of scenery. I needed to clear my mind. And I needed a fresh start - for myself, my son, and for Lauren because despite everything, I never once stopped believing in her or our family.

My mind wandered as Gregory and I drove down that long, vacant road. As he napped in the backseat, I imagined sharing the front seat with Lauren, like I did any other time we embarked on a new adventure together.

"Are you sure we're going the right way?" I heard her ask as the tires treaded through dirt and gravel - a question she always asked because she was never any good with maps or directions to destinations she'd never heard of before.

But as I extended my right arm across the front passenger

seat to protect her from the unexpected bump in the road, I was reminded that I was alone, as I had imagined she felt. But no matter what secrets the future kept, the present was what mattered then. As I pulled into the abandoned driveway —a shanty swallowed by an abundance of weeds— I couldn't help but wonder if I had made the right decision. It was far from Lauren's style, but I knew her well enough to believe that she'd say it was vintage. And she loved vintage. I could've turned back around, paid cash for the house two subdivisions down, and dealt with things in a different way. But what did I really have to turn back for? So, I moved forward.

That night, as I went through Lauren's things, trying to figure out how she might like them placed or if I should just leave them how they were until she came home, I stumbled across the manuscript of the novel she started while she was pregnant with Holly. I stayed up all night reading it and shedding tears for shit that I couldn't believe I was reading - shit that I had gone through with her in the last few months and shit that I had no idea she had gone through without me. In that moment, the only person I could think to reach out to was Tanya, her manager, so the next morning, that's what I did, hoping that my baby's art could somehow bring her back to me.

* * *

When I received the call from Tanya telling me that my book had been published, that it was a bestseller, and that I had just won The Pulitzer Prize for it, I was astounded. To be completely honest, I don't remember writing most of what ended up being in that book. However, I'm glad that I wrote it because my memory of the monster I became is quite hazy, and if I weren't where I am today, I wouldn't believe the words within those chapters. They're frightening. Unnerving. And they speak a truth that *feels* foreign to me... a truth that feels foreign to the professionals as well, as they struggle to narrow down my exact diagnosis. In the meantime, they keep my meds, *and me* close by. To manage my symptoms, you know?

When Tanya told me that a producer was interested in interviewing me and those closest to me because she wanted to adapt my work into a screenplay, I felt obligated to agree to it. After all that I had put my family through, the least I could do was give them a chance to tell their sides of the story, if they were willing to come forward, of course. And well, here we are... you and I exploring the facts of life which brought us together, aren't we?

Make no mistake: Living inside of these walls is quite isolating. While the rest of the world progresses, *we* are prisoners of our own minds until we decide to break free, which is the tricky part. Because in order to break free, one must first recognize that they aren't already. Maybe that's why I'm still here...

Because some days I have no doubt that my life hasn't concluded. I close my eyes and imagine being surrounded by a field of lavender lilies. Sometimes I even pretend that I'm one of them. Beautiful, peaceful, wild and free. And other days, I just want to lock the door and bury myself inside with the other oddities who hold no judgment. But then, I remember what my grandmother, Ivory used to say: "Even lavender lilies wither sometimes. But if you're patient and careful with them, they'll come back around." So, maybe someday I will.

www.ingramcontent.com/pod-product-compliance
Lightning Source LLC
Chambersburg PA
CBHW031535310726
48971CB00008B/2486